Dial-a-Ghost

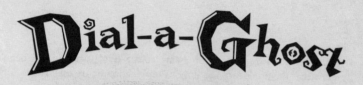

Dial-a-Ghost

Eva Ibbotson

ILLUSTRATED BY

Kevin Hawkes

SCHOLASTIC INC.

New York Toronto London Auckland Sydney
Mexico City New Delhi Hong Kong Buenos Aires

ISBN 0-439-44165-X

Text copyright © 1996 by Eva Ibbotson.
Illustrations copyright © 2001 by Kevin Hawkes. All rights reserved.
Published by Scholastic Inc., 557 Broadway, New York, NY 10012,
by arrangement with Dutton Children's Books, a member of
Penguin Putnam Inc. SCHOLASTIC and associated logos are
trademarks and/or registered trademarks of Scholastic Inc.

12 11 10 9 8 7 6 5 4 3 2   2 3 4 5 6 7/0

Printed in the U.S.A.   40

First Scholastic printing, October 2002

Typography by Richard Amari

Snodde-Brittle

I Set My Foot Upon My Enemies

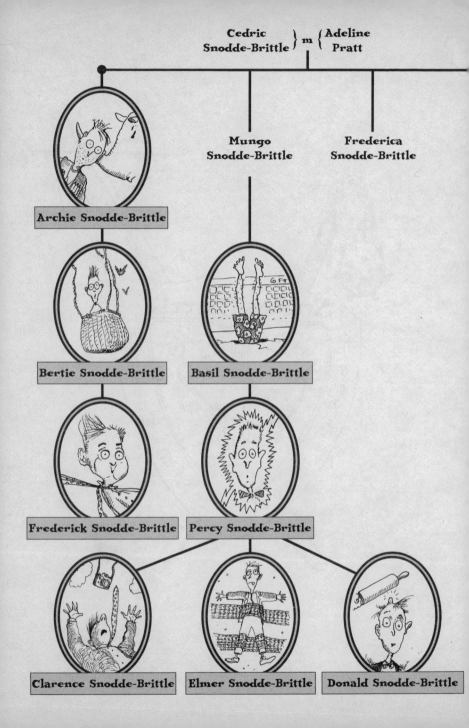

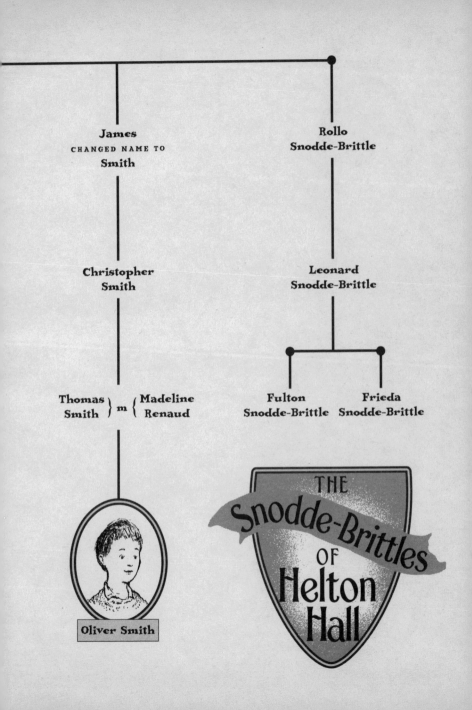

James
CHANGED NAME TO
Smith

Rollo
Snodde-Brittle

Christopher
Smith

Leonard
Snodde-Brittle

Thomas
Smith } m { Madeline
Renaud

Fulton
Snodde-Brittle

Frieda
Snodde-Brittle

Oliver Smith

THE
Snodde-Brittles
OF
Helton
Hall

Dial-a-Ghost

. Chapter 1 .

THE WILKINSON FAMILY became ghosts quite suddenly during the Second World War when a bomb fell on their house.

The house was called Resthaven, after the hotel where Mr. and Mrs. Wilkinson had spent their honeymoon, and you couldn't have found a nicer place to live. It had bow windows and a blue front door and stained glass in the bathroom and a garden with a bird table and a lily pond. Mrs. Wilkinson kept everything spotless. Her husband, Mr. Wilkinson, was a dentist who went to town every day to fill people's teeth, and they had a son called Eric, who was thirteen when the bomb fell. He was a Boy Scout and had just started having spots and falling in love with girls who sneered at him.

Also living in the house were Mrs. Wilkinson's mother, who was a fierce old lady with a dangerous umbrella, and Mrs. Wilkinson's sister Trixie, a pale, fluttery person to whom bad things were always happening.

The family had been getting ready to go to the air-raid shelter at the bottom of the garden, and they were collecting the things they needed. Grandma took her umbrella and her gas mask case, which did not hold her gas mask but a bottle labeled POISON. She meant to drink it if there was an invasion rather than fall into enemy hands. Mrs. Wilkinson gathered up her knitting and unhooked the birdcage that held their pet bird, a budgie, and Eric took a book called *Scouting for Boys* and the letter he was writing to a girl called Cynthia Harbottle.

In the hall they met Mr. Wilkinson, who had just come in and was changing into his khaki uniform. He belonged to the Home Guard, a brave band of part-time soldiers who practiced crawling through the undergrowth and shooting things when they had finished work.

"Hurry up, everyone," he said. "The planes are getting closer."

But just then, they remembered that poor Trixie was still in her upstairs bedroom wrapped in a flag. The flag was her costume for a show the Women's Institute was putting on for the gallant soldiers, and Trixie had been chosen to be the Spirit of Britain and to come on in the flag, the Union Jack.

"I'll just go and fetch her," said Mrs. Wilkinson, who knew that Trixie had not been at all happy with the way she looked and might be too shy to come down and join them.

She began to climb the stairs . . . and then the bomb fell, and that was that.

• • •

Of course it was a shock realizing that they had suddenly become ghosts.

"Fancy me a spook!" said Grandma, shaking her head.

Still, there they were—a bit pale and shimmery, of course, but not looking so different from the way they had before. Grandma always wore her best hat to the shelter, the one with the bunch of cherries trimmed with lover's knots, and the whiskers on her chin stuck out like daggers in the moonlight. Eric was in his Scout uniform with the scarf and the badge to show that he was a Pathfinder, and his spectacles were still on his nose. Only the budgie didn't look too good. He had lost his tail feathers and seemed to have become rather a *small* bird.

"Oh Henry, what shall we do now?" asked Mrs. Wilkinson. The top half of her husband was dressed like a soldier in a tin hat that he had covered with leaves so as to make himself look like a bush, but the bottom half was dressed like a dentist. Mrs. Wilkinson, who loved him very much, glided close to him and looked up into his face.

"We shall do what we did before, Maud," said Mr. Wilkinson. "Live decent lives and serve our country."

"At least we're all together," said Grandma.

But then a terrible silence fell, and as the specters looked at each other, their ectoplasm turned as white as snow.

"Where is Trixie?" Mrs. Wilkinson faltered. "Where is my dear sister?"

Where indeed? They searched what was left of the house, they searched the garden, they called and called, but there was no sign of a shy spook with spectacles dressed in nothing but a flag.

For poor Maud Wilkinson, this was an awful blow. She cried, she moaned, she wrung her hands. "I promised Mother I would look after her," she wailed. "I've always looked after Trixie."

This was true. Maud and Trixie's mother had run a stage dancing school, and ever since they were little, Maud had helped her nervous sister be a Sugar Puff or a Baby Swan or a Dandelion.

But there was nothing to be done. Why some people become ghosts and others don't is a mystery that no one has ever solved.

. . .

The next years passed uneventfully. The war ended, but nobody came to rebuild their house, and the Wilkinsons lived in it much as they had done before. It was completely ruined, but they could remember where all the rooms were, and in a way, being a ghost is simple; you don't feel the cold or have to go to school, and they soon got the hang of passing through walls and vanishing. Having Mr. Wilkinson to explain things to them was a great help, of course.

"You have to remember," he said, "that while people are made of muscle and skin and bone, ghosts are made of ectoplasm. But that does not mean," he went on sternly, "that we can allow ourselves to become feeble and woozy and faint. Ectoplasm can be strengthened just the way that muscles can."

But however busy they were doing knee bends and press-ups and learning to move things by the power of their will, they never forgot poor Trixie. Every single evening, as the sun went down, they went into the garden and called her. They called her from the north, they called her from the south and the east and the west, but the sad, goose-pimpled spook never appeared.

Then, when they had been phantoms for about fifteen years, something unexpected happened. They found the ghost of a lost child.

They were out for an early morning glide in the fields near their house when they saw a white shape lying in the grass, under the shelter of a hedge.

"Goodness, do you think it's a passed-on sheep?" asked Mrs. Wilkinson.

But when they got closer they saw that it was not the ghost of a sheep that lay there. It was the ghost of a little girl. She wore an old-fashioned nightdress with a ribbon round the neck and one embroidered slipper, and though she was fast asleep, the string of a rubber sponge bag was clasped in her hand.

"She must be a ghost from olden times," said Mrs. Wilkinson excitedly. "Look at the stitching on that night-dress! You don't get sewing like that nowadays."

"She looks wet," said Grandma.

This was true. Drops of water glistened in her long, tousled hair and her one bare foot looked damp.

"Perhaps she drowned?" suggested Eric.

Mr. Wilkinson opened the sponge bag. Inside it were the expected toiletries: a toothbrush, a tin of tooth pow-der with a picture of Queen Victoria on the lid, and . . . a fish. It was a wild fish, not the kind that lives in tanks, but it, too, was a ghost, and could tell them nothing.

"It must have floated into the sponge bag when she was in the water," said Mr. Wilkinson.

But the thing to do now was to wake the child, and this was difficult. She didn't seem to be just asleep; she seemed to be in a coma.

In the end, it was the budgie who did it by saying, "Open wide" in his high squawking voice. He had learned to say this when his cage hung in the dentist's office, because it was what Mr. Wilkinson said to his patients when they sat down in the dentist's chair.

"Oh, the sweet thing!" cried Mrs. Wilkinson as the child stirred and stretched. "Isn't she a darling! I'm sure she's lost, and if she is, she must come and make her home with us, mustn't she, Henry? We must adopt her!" She bent over the child. "What's your name, dear? Can you remember what you're called?"

The girl's eyes were open now, but she was still not properly awake. "Adopt . . . her," she repeated. And then in a stronger voice, "Adopta."

"Adopta," repeated Mrs. Wilkinson. "That's an odd name . . . but very pretty."

So that was what she came to be called, though they often called her Addie for short. She never remembered anything about her past life, and Mr. Wilkinson, who knew things, said she had had a concussion, which is a blow on the head that makes you forget your past. Mr. and Mrs. Wilkinson never pretended to be her parents (she was told to call them Uncle Henry and Aunt Maud), but she hadn't been with them for more than a few weeks before they felt that she was the daughter they had always longed for—and the greatest comfort in the troubled times that now began.

Because life now became very difficult. Their house was rebuilt, and the people who moved in were the kind who couldn't see ghosts. They thought nothing of putting a plate of scrambled eggs down on Grandma's head, or running the Hoover over the carpet and through Eric when he wanted to be quiet and think about why Cynthia Harbottle didn't love him.

And when they left, another set of people moved in who *could* see ghosts, and that was even worse. Every time any of the Wilkinsons appeared, they shrieked and screamed and fainted, which was terribly hurtful.

"I could understand it if we were headless," said Aunt Maud. "I'd *expect* to be screamed at if I was headless."

"Or bloodstained," agreed Grandma. "But we have always kept ourselves decent and the children, too."

Then the new people stopped screaming and started talking about getting the ghosts exorcized, and after that there was nothing for it. They left their beloved Resthaven and went away to find another home.

. Chapter 2 .

THE WILKINSONS WENT to London thinking there would be a lot of empty houses there, but this was a mistake. No place had been more bombed in the war, and it was absolutely packed with ghosts. Ghosts in swimming pools and ghosts in schools, ghosts whooping about in bus stations, ghosts in factories and offices, playing about with computers. And older ghosts, too, from a bygone age: knights in armor wandering round Indian take-aways, wailing nuns in toy shops, and all of them looking completely flaked out and muddled.

In the end, the Wilkinsons found a shopping arcade that didn't seem too crowded. It had all sorts of shops in it: shoe shops and grocer's shops and sweet shops and a bunion shop, which puzzled Adopta.

"Can you *buy* bunions, Aunt Maud?" she asked, looking at the big wooden foot in the window with a leather bunion nailed to one toe.

"No, dear. Bunions are nasty bumps that people get on the side of their toes. But you can buy things to make bunions better, like medicated pads and ointments."

But the bunion shop, which was really a hospital-supply shop, was already haunted by a frail ghost called Mr. Hofmann, a German professor who had made himself quite ill by looking at the bowls for spitting into, and the rubber tubes, and the wall charts showing what could go wrong with people's livers . . . which was plenty.

So they went to live in a knicker shop.

Adopta called it the Knicker Shop, but of course no one can make a living just by selling underpants. It sold pajamas and swimsuits and nightdresses and undershirts, but none of them were at all like the pajamas and swim-suits and undershirts the Wilkinsons were used to.

"In my days, knickers were long and decent, with elastic at the knee and pockets to keep your hankie in," grumbled Grandma. "And those bikinis! I was twenty-five before I saw my first tummy button, and look at those hussies in the fitting rooms. Shameless, I call it."

"It's the children I'm bothered about," said Aunt Maud. "They shouldn't be seeing such things."

And really, some of the clothes sold in that shop were *not* nice!—garter belts that were just a row of frills and see-through slips and transparent boxes full of briefs.

"Brief whats?" snorted Grandma.

Still, they really tried to settle down and make a life for themselves. Adopta was put to sleep in the office, where she wouldn't be among ruffled panties and tights with rude names, and Uncle Henry stayed among the socks because there is a limit to how silly you can get with socks. They hung the budgie's cage on the rack beside the Wonderbras and told themselves that they were lucky to have a roof over their heads at all.

But they were not happy. The shopping arcade was stuffy, and the people wandering up and down it looked greedy and bored. They missed the garden at Resthaven and the green fields, and although they went out and called Trixie every night, they couldn't help wondering whether a shy person dressed in a flag would dare to appear in such a crowded place even if she heard them.

Aunt Maud did everything she could to make the knicker shop into a proper home for ghosts. She arranged cobwebs on the ceiling and brought in dead thistles from the graveyard and rubbed mold into the walls, but the lady who sold the knickers was a demon with the floor polisher. She was another one who couldn't see ghosts, and though they slept all day and tried to keep out of her way, she was forever barging through them or spinning the poor budgie round as she twiddled the Wonderbras on their stand. Grandma was getting bothered about Mr. Hofmann in the bunion shop—he kept coming up with more and more diseases—and Eric had started counting his spots again and writing awful poetry to Cynthia Harbottle.

"But, Eric, we've been ghosts for years and years!" his mother would cry. "Cynthia'd be a fat old lady by now."

But this only hurt Eric, who said that to him she would always be young, and he would glide off to the greeting-card shop to see if he could find anything to rhyme with Cynthia, or Harbottle, or both.

"Oh, Henry, do you think we shall ever have a proper home again?" poor Maud would cry. And her husband would pat her back and tell her to be patient, and never let on that when he was pretending to go to the dental hospital to study new ways of filling teeth, he was really house-hunting, and had found nothing at all.

But Aunt Maud's worst worry was about Adopta. Addie was becoming a street ghost. She often stayed out all night, and she was picking up bad habits and mixing with completely the wrong sort of ghost: ghosts who had been having a bath when their house caught fire and hadn't had time to put on any clothes; the ghosts of rat-catchers and vulgar people who swore and drank in pubs.

And she was bringing in the most unsuitable pets.

Addie had always been crazy about animals. She liked living animals, but, of course, for a ghost to drag living animals about is silly, and the ones that held her heart were the creatures that had passed on and become ghosts and didn't quite understand what had happened to them. But it was one thing to fill the garden at Resthaven with phantom hedgehogs and rabbits and moles, and quite another to keep a run-over alley cat or a battered pigeon among the satin pajamas and the leotards.

"Please, dear, no more strays," begged Aunt Maud. "After all, you have the budgie and your dear fish."

But though she wouldn't have hurt Aunt Maud for the world, Addie couldn't help feeling that a bird who said nothing but "Open wide" and "My name is Billie" wasn't very interesting. Nor was her fish much fun. He stayed in the sponge bag and did absolutely nothing, and though Adopta didn't blame him, she longed for an exciting pet. Something unusual.

So she began to haunt London Zoo, and it was on the way back from there one winter's night that she saw something that was to change all their lives.

She had had her eye on a duck-billed platypus that had not looked at all well the day before. Its brown fur looked limp and dull, its eyes were filmed over, and its big flat beak seemed to be covered in some kind of mold. Of course she knew that even if it died, the duck-bill would not necessarily become a ghost—animals are the same as people: some become ghosts and some don't. Even so, as she glided toward its cage, Adopta was full of hope. She imagined taking it to bed with her, holding it in her arms. No one had such an unusual pet, and though Aunt Maud would make a fuss at the beginning, she was far too kind to turn it out into the street.

But a great disappointment awaited her. The silly keeper must have given the duckbill some medicine, because it looked much better. In fact, it looked fine; it was lumbering round the cage like a two-year-old and eating a worm.

Perhaps it was because she was so sad about her lost pet that she took a wrong turning on the way home to the knicker shop. The street she was gliding down was not the one she went down usually. She was just about to turn back when she saw a sign above a tall gray house. It was picked out in blue electric lightbulbs, and what it said was:

ADOPTA GHOST

Addie braked hard and stared at it. She was utterly amazed. "But that is extraordinary," she said. "That is *my* name. I'm called Adopta and I'm a ghost."

She floated up to the roof and stared at the letters. "Is it my house?" she wondered. "Is it a house for me?"

But that didn't seem very likely. Could there be *two* Adopta Ghosts in the world? Was this the home of a very grand spook with green skin and hollow eyes; a queenly spook with trailing dresses ordering everyone about? But when she peered through the windows, she saw that

the rooms looked rather dull—offices with files and desks and telephones. A queenly spook with green ectoplasm would never live in a place like that.

Very much excited, Addie hurried home.

"Aunt Maud, you must come at *once*," she said. "I've seen the most amazing thing!"

"Addie, it's your bedtime; it's nearly eight in the morning. They'll be opening the shop in half an hour."

"Please," begged Adopta. "I just know this is important!"

So Maud came and landed on the ledge beneath the notice, and when she had done so, she was quite as excited as the child had been.

"My dear, it doesn't say 'Adopta Ghost.' Look carefully and you'll see a space between the middle letters. It says 'Adopt-a-Ghost.' And I really believe it's an agency to find homes for people like us. Look, there's a notice: *Ghosts wanting to be rehoused should register between midnight and 3 A.M. on Tuesdays, Thursdays, or Saturdays.*"

She turned to the child and hugged her. "Oh Addie, I do believe our troubles are over. There is someone who cares about us—someone who really and truly cares!"

. Chapter 3 .

AUNT MAUD WAS RIGHT. There *was* someone who cared about ghosts and who cared about them very much. Two people to be exact: Miss Pringle, who was small and twittery with round blue eyes, and Mrs. Mannering, who was big and bossy and wore jackets with huge shoulder pads and had a booming voice.

The two ladies had met at an evening class for witches. They were interested in unusual ways of living, and thought they might have Special Powers, which would have been nice. But they hadn't enjoyed the classes at all. They were held in a basement near Paddington Station, and the other people there had wanted to do things that Miss Pringle and Mrs. Mannering could not possibly approve of, things like dancing counterclockwise dressed in nothing but their underclothes and sticking pins into puppets that had taken some poor person a long time to make.

All the same, the classes must have done some good, because afterward both the ladies found that they were much better than they had been before at seeing ghosts.

They had always been able to see ghosts in a vague and shimmery way, but now they saw them as clearly as if they were ordinary people—and the ladies did not like what they saw.

There were ghosts eating their hearts out in cinemas and bottle factories; there were headless warriors in all-night garages, and bloodstained brides who rode round and round the underground because they had nowhere to sleep.

And it was then they got the idea for the agency. For after all, if people can adopt whales and trees in rain forests, if schoolchildren can adopt London buses and crocodiles in the zoo—why not ghosts? Only they would have to be proper adoptions, not just sending money. Ghosts, after all, are not whales or crocodiles; they can fit perfectly well into the right sort of house.

"There might be people who would be only too happy to have a ghost or two in their stately home to attract tourists," said Miss Pringle.

"And they'd be splendid for keeping off burglars," said Mrs. Mannering.

So they decided to start an agency and call it Dial-a-Ghost. Miss Pringle had some money and was glad to spend it in such a useful way. She was a very kind person but a little vague, and it was Mrs. Mannering who knew what to do about furnishing the office and getting filing cabinets and putting out leaflets. It was she, too, who arranged for separate doors, one saying GHOSTS and one saying PEOPLE, and printed the notice explaining that they would see ghosts on Tuesdays, Thursdays, and Saturdays, and people who wanted to adopt them on the other days. And it was she who had ordered the electric signs, one saying DIAL-A-GHOST, and the other saying ADOPT-A-GHOST, just to be perfectly clear.

But it was kind, dithery Miss Pringle who engaged the office boy. He was called Ted and she gave him the job because he looked hungry and his parents were out of work. He was a nice boy, but there was something he hadn't told the ladies . . . and this "something" turned out to be important.

• • •

After the agency had been going for a few months, Miss Pringle and Mrs. Mannering began to specialize. Miss Pringle dealt with the gentle, peaceful ghosts—the sad ladies who had been left at the altar on their wedding days and jumped off cliffs, and the cold, white little children who had fallen off roofs in their boarding schools, and so on. And Mrs. Mannering coped with the fierce ones—the ones who were livid and revolting and rattled their chains.

And every evening when they had finished work, the two ladies went to a pub called the Dirty Duck and ordered a port wine and lemon and told each other how their day had gone.

"I had such a delightful family in just now," said Miss Pringle. "The Wilkinsons. I just must fix them up with somewhere to go, and quickly."

"I think I saw them. Not bloodstained at all, as I recall?" said Mrs. Mannering.

"No, not at all. You could say ordinary, but in the best sense of the word. They told me such interesting things about the war. Mrs. Wilkinson used to stand in line for three hours just for one banana, and the old lady once held down an enemy parachutist with her umbrella till the police came to take him away. And there is such a dear little girl. She wasn't born a Wilkinson, they found her lost and abandoned. She could be anyone—a princess even."

"It shouldn't be difficult to find them a home if they're so nice."

"No. Except that there are five of them; I don't seem to have anyone on my books who'll take as many as that. They've had such trouble in their lives—there was a sister . . ." She told the sad story of Trixie and the flag. "And Mrs. Wilkinson is so worried about her son. Apparently he was really clever—the top of his class and a patrol leader in the Scouts—and then he got mixed up with this dreadful girl who cadged chewing gum from the American soldiers and sneered at him. It seems to me so wrong, Dorothy, that a family who gave their lives for their country should have to haunt a knicker shop." She looked across at her friend and saw that Mrs. Mannering was looking very tired. "My dear, how selfish of me! You had the Shriekers in, didn't you? I saw Ted going to hide in the lavatory . . . and the poor geranium is still completely black."

"Yes." Mrs. Mannering was a big, strong woman, but she sat with her shoulders hunched and she had hardly tasted her drink. "I really don't know what to do, Nellie. They're so rude and noisy and ungrateful. If it wasn't for the way they carry on about children, I might find them a place—after all, they're nobly born, and people like that."

"We can't have them hurting children, that's true," said Miss Pringle. "I wonder what made them the way they are? I gather even the sight of a healthy child drives them quite mad?"

Mrs. Mannering nodded. "There's nothing they wouldn't do to children: slash their faces, strangle them in their bedclothes, set fire to them." She sighed. "I'm not mealymouthed, Nellie, you know that. If someone comes to me with his head under his arm and says 'Find me a home,' I'll say 'Fair enough.' I've fixed up spooks who played 'Chopsticks' with their toe bones; I've fixed up moaners and I've fixed up dribblers—but I won't take any risks with children. I really think we'll have to cross the Shriekers off our books."

Miss Pringle shuddered. "I wouldn't like to make an enemy of the Shriekers."

"No." Even Mrs. Mannering, tough as she was, didn't like the idea of that. "Well, we'll give it a bit longer. Perhaps something will turn up."

• • •

The Shriekers were a most appalling pair of spooks. They weren't just violent and cruel and fiendish, they were snobbish as well. Nothing on earth would have made the Shriekers haunt anything as humble as a knicker shop. They lived in a frozen meat store on the other side of the city.

It was a dreadful place, but the Shriekers didn't mind the strings of sausages that fastened round their throats as they glided about, or the tubs of greasy white lard, or the sides of cut-up animals hanging from hooks in the ceiling. They were so filthy and loathsome themselves that they hardly noticed the stench or the cold or the slime on the floor.

Once it had not been so. When they were alive, the Shriekers had been rather a grand couple. Their names were Sir Pelham and Lady Sabrina de Bone, and they lived in a fortified tower beside a lake. Sir Pelham rode to hounds and shot pheasants, and Sabrina wore fine clothes and gave dinner parties and kept a house full of servants. In fact, they were so important that Queen Victoria once came to stay with them on her way to Scotland.

But when they had been married for about ten years, the de Bones had a Great Sorrow and this had driven them mad. No one knew what their sorrow was; they never spoke about it, and the grief and guilt of it had turned inward and made them wilder and crazier with every year that passed. Even before they became ghosts, people had been terrified of the de Bones, and now the sight of them sent the strongest man running for cover. Sir Pelham still wore the jodhpurs and hunting jacket he had worn when he broke his neck, but they were covered with filth and gore and he carried a long-thonged whip with which he slashed at everything that crossed his path. His forehead had been bashed in by a horse's hoof, so that it was just a mass of splintered bone; his left ear hung by a thread; and through the rents in his trousers you could see his scarred and vicious knees.

His wife was even worse. Sabrina's dress was so blood-stained that you couldn't see the fabric underneath, and hatred had worn away two of her toes and her nose, which was nothing but a nibbled stump. She had picked up a phantom python on her travels and wore it slung round her neck, so that the evil-smelling eggs it laid broke and dribbled down inside her undershirt. Worst of all were her long fingernails, from which bits of skin and hair stuck out because of the tearing and scratching she did all day.

Not only were the Shriekers hateful to look at, but they were the most foulmouthed couple you could imagine. You could hear them shouting abuse at each other from the moment they woke up to the moment they went to bed.

"Do you call that blood!" Sabrina would shriek when her husband dripped some gore onto the ground. "Why that isn't even tomato ketchup! I could put that on my dinner of fish fingers and not even notice it, you slime-grub!"

"Don't you dare call me names, you maggot-ridden cowpat," Sir Pelham would yell back. "What have *you* done today, I'd like to know? You were going to strangle the butcher's boy before lunch and there isn't a mark on him. And your python looks perfectly ridiculous. You've tied it in a granny knot. Pythons should be tied in a *reef* knot, everyone knows that."

The only time the Shriekers were cheerful was when they were working out something awful to do to children. When they had thought of some new way of harming a child, Sabrina would open one of the meat containers and take out a pig's trotter to put in her hair, and string a row of pork chops together to make a belt for her husband, and they would do a stately dance in the dark, cold room so that one could see how proud and grand they had once been.

But it never lasted long. Soon they'd tear everything off again and bombard each other with pieces of liver and start screaming for more horror and more blood.

The Shriekers had a servant, a miserable, gray, jellylike creature; a ghoul whom they had found asleep in a graveyard with a rope round his neck. He slept behind a waste bin, and every so often they would kick him awake and tell him to cook something, and he would totter about muttering, "Sizzle" or "Roast" or "Burn," and swipe vaguely at the sausages with a frying pan. But the cold had almost done him in—ghouls are not suitable for freezing—and the thought of doing their own housework made the Shriekers absolutely furious with the kind ladies of the adoption agency.

"Those human blisters," yelled Sir Pelham, "those suppurating boils!"

"I bet they're lying in their beds snoring while we rot in this hellhole," shouted Sabrina.

But the Shriekers were wrong. At that very moment, though it was late at night, Miss Pringle and Mrs. Mannering were putting one hundred leaflets into brown envelopes and sticking on one hundred stamps. The leaflets were addressed to the owners of grand houses and stately homes all over Britain, and offered ghosts of every kind suitable for adoption straightaway.

And two days later, one of those leaflets dropped onto the dusty, marble floor of Helton Hall.

. Chapter 4 .

ELTON HALL WAS a large, grand, and rather gloomy house in the north of England. It was built of gray stone and had a gray slate roof, and gray stone statues of gods and goddesses with chipped and snooty-looking faces lined the terrace. Helton had thirteen bedrooms, and stables and outhouses and a lake in which a farmer had once drowned himself. At the end of the long gray gravel drive was a large iron gate with spikes on it, the kind you could have stuck people's heads on in the olden days, and on top of the pillars sat two carved griffons with evil-looking eyes and vicious beaks.

Helton had belonged for hundreds of years to a family by the name of Snodde-Brittle. They owned not just the house but most of the village and a farm and they were very proud of their name, though you might think that a name like Snodde-Brittle was nothing to be cocky about. Their family motto was "I Set My Foot Upon

My Enemies," and if any Snodde-Brittle tried to marry someone who was common and didn't speak "nicely," they were banished from Helton Hall.

But then things began to go wrong for the Snodde-Brittles. Old Archie Snodde-Brittle, who liked to hunt big game, was run through by a rhinoceros. Then his son, Bertie Snodde-Brittle, took up hot-air ballooning and was shot down by a madwoman who thought he was a space invader, and Bertie's son, Frederick, was strangled by his tie. (He had been chasing a housemaid in the laundry room and his tie had got caught between the rollers in the mangle, an ironing machine.)

Helton then passed to a cousin of Bertie's who was not very bright and dived into a swimming pool without noticing that it was not filled with water, and the cousin's son was struck by lightning when he went to shelter under the only tree for miles around that was sticking straight up into the air.

Fortunately the cousin's son had had time to marry and have children, but the luck of the Snodde-Brittles was still out. The eldest son fell off a cliff while robbing an eagle's nest in Scotland; the next one crashed while passing an oil tanker round a blind bend in the road; and the youngest was hit on the head with a rolling pin by an old lady he was trying to turn out of her cottage on the estate.

That was the end of that particular batch of Brittles,

and the lawyers now had to search the family tree to find out who should inherit next. It looked as though it would be a man called Fulton Snodde-Brittle, who was the grandson of Archie's youngest brother, Rollo. Fulton had watched eagerly as the ruling Snodde-Brittles were struck by lightning and dived into empty swimming pools and had their heads bashed in by fierce old ladies. But just as he was getting ready to come to Helton, a most exciting discovery was made.

It seemed that Archie had had another brother called James, who was older than Rollo. James had quarreled with his family and changed his name and gone to live abroad, but it now turned out that James's great-grandson was still alive. He was an orphan, not more than ten years old, and had spent most of his life in a children's home in London.

The name of this boy was Oliver Smith, and there was no doubt at all that he was the true and rightful owner of Helton Hall.

The news soon spread all over Helton Village.

"It's like a fairy story!" said the blacksmith's wife.

"Imagine his little face when they tell him!" said the lady in the post office.

Even the family lawyer, Mr. Norman, and the bank manager who was a trustee for the estate were amazed.

"It's really extraordinary," said the bank manager. "A

child brought up in an orphanage. One wonders how he will be able to cope. I suppose there's no doubt about who he is?"

"None at all. I've checked all his papers. We'll have to appoint a guardian, of course." The lawyer sighed. It was going to make a lot of work, putting a child into Helton Hall.

. . .

The Lexington Children's Home was in a shabby part of London, beside a railway line and a factory that made parts for washing machines and fridges. The building was grimy, and the beds the children slept in were old bunk beds bought from the army years and years ago. Instead of soft carpets on the floor, there were hard tiles, some of them chipped; the chairs were rickety and the only telly was so old that you couldn't really tell whether the pictures were meant to be black-and-white or in color.

But there was something odd about the Home and it was this: the children who lived there didn't want to be adopted.

When there was talk of someone coming to foster a child and take him or her away, the children slunk off to various hiding places, or they pretended to be ill, and the naughty ones lay down on the floor and drummed their heels. People from outside couldn't understand this, but it was perfectly simple really. The Home might be shabby and poor, but it was a happy place; it was their place. It was where they belonged.

The children came from all sorts of backgrounds, but there was something a little bit wrong with most of them, and perhaps that made them kinder to each other than if they'd been big and blustering and tough. Harry stammered so badly you could hardly tell what he was saying, and Trevor had lost a hand in the accident that killed his parents. Nonie still wet her bed though she was nearly ten, and Tabitha couldn't help stealing; things just got into her locker and wouldn't come out.

And Oliver, who knew himself only as Oliver Smith, suffered from asthma; he'd had it since his parents died when he was three years old. The doctor said he'd probably grow out of it, but he hadn't yet, and it could be scary, not being able to catch one's breath.

Most of the time, though, Oliver was fine. There were things in the Lexington Children's Home that made up for all the shabbiness and the rattling of the trains and the smell from the factory chimneys. Behind the house was a piece of ground where every single child who wanted to could have a little garden. Matron had saved a three-legged mongrel from a road smash—a brave and intelligent dog who lived with them—and they kept bantam hens that did not lay eggs very often but sometimes. Trevor had a guinea pig and Nonie had a rabbit and Durga had a minah bird she had taught to sing a rude song in Urdu.

Best of all, the children had each other. You never had to be alone in the Home. At night in the bunk beds, there were stories told and plans hatched, and if Matron couldn't come to a crying child, there was usually someone who got in beside the child who was miserable and made him laugh.

To Oliver, the other children were his brothers and sisters; Matron, if she couldn't come near to being his mother, was kind and fair. There was no dog like Sparky, racing round on her three legs, no conkers like the ones they shook down from the old chestnut tree on the embankment—and when the mustard and cress came up on his patch of garden and he could make sandwiches for everyone for tea, he was as pleased as if he'd won first prize at the Chelsea Flower Show.

So you can imagine how he felt on the day that Matron led him into her office and told him that he was not Oliver Smith but Oliver Snodde-Brittle and the new owner of Helton Hall.

Though she spoke slowly and carefully, Oliver at first thought that she must be joking—except that she wasn't a person who teased people, and if this was a joke it was a very cruel one.

"It will be a fine chance for you, Oliver," she said. "In a place like that, you'll be able to help people and do so much good."

She tried to smile at the little boy staring at her in

horror out of his large dark eyes. He did not look very much like the master of a stately home, with his sticklike arms and legs and his soft fawn hair.

"You mean I have to go miles and miles away and live by myself?"

"You won't be by yourself for long. Some cousins are coming to fetch you and help you settle in. Think of it, Oliver—you'll be in the country and able to have all the animals you want. Ponies . . . a dog . . ."

"I don't want any dog but Sparky. I don't want to go away. Please don't make me go. *Please!*"

Matron took him in her arms. She had never told children that it was sissy to cry—sometimes one cried and that was the end of it—and now as she smoothed back Oliver's hair, she felt his tears run down her hand.

As a matter of fact, she didn't feel too good herself. She made it a rule not to have favorites, but she loved this boy; he was imaginative and kind and funny and she was going to miss him horribly.

And she wasn't the only one. There was going to be a nasty fuss when Oliver's friends heard he was leaving. A very nasty fuss indeed.

• • •

The cousins who were coming to fetch Oliver were called Fulton and Frieda Snodde-Brittle. Fulton was the headmaster of a boys' prep school in Yorkshire and

Frieda was his sister, and they had sent a letter to the lawyer, Mr. Norman, offering to take charge of him.

Our school will be shut for the Easter holidays, Fulton had written, *and we shall be happy to help him settle in. It must be rather a shock for the poor little fellow. As you know, we are used to boys; the pupils in our care are just like our own children, and we shall know how to make him comfortable.*

"I must say that's very kind," said Mr. Norman, showing the letter to the bank manager. "I was going to go and fetch Oliver myself, but I'm very busy. And really I didn't know what was going to be done with the child in that barracks of a place. It's been shut up for months and the servants are very old."

"You haven't heard from Colonel Mersham?" asked the bank manager.

Mr. Norman shook his head. The man they had chosen to be Oliver's guardian was an explorer and away in Costa Rica looking for a rare breed of golden toad.

"He's due back at the end of the summer, but in the meantime this offer of Fulton's is most convenient."

"Yes. I must say he's been very decent when you think that if it weren't for Oliver, Fulton himself would be master of Helton Hall."

Which just shows how simpleminded lawyers and bank managers can sometimes get.

• • •

Because Fulton wasn't kind at all—he was evil, and so was his sister Frieda. The school that they ran was called Sunnydell, but no place could have been less sunny. The children were beaten, the food was unedible, and the classrooms were freezing. The sweets the parents sent were confiscated, and the letters the boys wrote home to say how miserable they were never got posted.

But you can only run a school like that for so long. The inspectors were getting wise to the Snodde-Brittles, and so were the parents. At first, they had liked the idea of their boys being toughened up, but gradually more and more children had been taken away, and as the school got smaller and smaller, the Snodde-Brittles got poorer and poorer.

So when they heard that the last owner of Helton had had his head bashed in by a fierce old lady, their joy knew no bounds.

"I'm the new master of Helton!" yelled Fulton.

"And I'm the new mistress!" shouted Frieda.

"We'll Set Our Foot Upon Our Enemies!" shouted Fulton.

"*Both* our feet!"

And then came the letter from the lawyer saying that Oliver had been found and that he and not Fulton was the rightful owner of Helton.

For two days, the Snodde-Brittles nearly choked

themselves with rage. They prowled the corridors muttering and cursing; they practiced every kind of cruelty on the pupils, twisting their arms, shutting them in cupboards; they shook their fists at the heavens.

Then Fulton calmed down. "Now listen, Frieda, there must be something we can do about this boy."

"Kill him, do you mean?" asked Frieda uneasily.

"No, no. Not directly. The police would get onto that; they've got all sorts of scientific equipment these days. But there'll be something. We've just got to show that he's unfit to take over . . . that he's mad or ill. There's bound to be bad blood in him somewhere. Now listen: we've got to pretend to be his friends . . . his loving relations," said Fulton with a leer. "We've got to show everyone that we're on his side—and then . . ."

"And then what?"

"I don't know yet. But I will soon. Just leave it to me."

So they wrote to the lawyer and two weeks later they were on their way to London.

• • •

"What a shabby house," said Frieda disgustedly as the taxi drew up in front of the Home. "The curtains are patched and the plaster is peeling. Really, I don't know what the city council is doing to allow such a place."

Both the Snodde-Brittles were dressed in black, both

were tall and bony, and both had mustaches. Fulton's mustache was there on purpose—a dung-colored growth on his upper lip. Frieda's was there by bad luck.

"One could hardly expect anything else in this part of London," said Fulton, not giving the taxi driver his tip and sneering at an old lady shuffling to the corner shop in her slippers. "It is given over to beggars and the poor. People who are shiftless and don't work."

The door was opened by a cheerful girl in a pink overall that Frieda disapproved of: maids should wear uniforms and call her "madam." She also disapproved of the rich smell of frying chips, the sound of laughter from the garden, and the children's paintings tacked to the walls of the corridor.

"Matron will be along in a minute," said the girl, and showed them into an office with two sagging armchairs and a large desk almost completely covered in photographs of children who had been in the Home throughout the years.

"It's quite extraordinary that a true Snodde-Brittle should have been living in a place such as this," said Frieda.

"If the brat *is* a true Snodde-Brittle," said Fulton, biting his mustache.

Matron came in. She wore a woolen skirt and a hand-knit cardigan, and clinging to her hand was a small boy.

"Good heavens!" said Frieda rudely. "Is *that* the child?"

"Yes, this is Oliver," said Matron quietly, giving his hand a squeeze.

"I do not see even a trace of the Snodde-Brittles in this boy," said Fulton, frowning.

This was true. The Snodde-Brittles were tall and long-faced, with bulging eyes and mouthfuls of enormous teeth.

"His mother was French," said Matron. "We think that Oliver takes after her."

"Ha!" Fulton was disgusted. Foreign blood! Then, remembering that he was posing as Oliver's friend, he leaned toward him and said: "Well now, boy, you will have heard of your good fortune?"

"Yes."

Oliver's voice was almost a whisper. His troubled eyes were turned to Matron.

"You don't seem to realize how lucky you are. Children all over the world would give anything to be in your shoes."

Oliver raised his head, suddenly looking cheerful. "If there are children all over the world who want to live there, can't I give it to them—Helton Hall, I mean—and stay here?"

"Stay here?" said Fulton.

"Stay *here?*" said Frieda.

The Snodde-Brittles were flabbergasted. They couldn't believe their ears.

"Oliver, you must try out your new life," said Matron. "We'll write you lots and lots of letters, and as soon as you're settled, some of the children will be able to come and stay."

The Snodde-Brittles looked at each other. Long before common and scruffy children were allowed to come and stay at Helton, Oliver should be safely out of the way.

"We have to catch the three-twenty from King's Cross Station," said Frieda.

Matron nodded. "Go and get your things, dear," she said to Oliver. "And tell the others that they can come and see you off."

When the boy had gone, she turned to the Snodde-Brittles. "You will find Oliver a willing and intelligent child," she said, "but he's delicate. When he's upset or if he gets some kind of shock, he has asthma attacks and finds it difficult to breathe. I've packed his inhaler and exact instructions about what to do, and of course you'll have a doctor up there. But the main thing is to keep him on an even keel, and happy. Then he's fine."

The Snodde-Brittles exchanged glances.

"Really?" said Fulton, licking his lips. "You mean it could be dangerous for him to have a shock? Really dangerous?"

"It could be," said Matron. "But if you're careful, everything will be fine. We've never had any trouble here."

In the taxi on the way to the station, Fulton was silent, thinking hard. A shock could be dangerous, could it? But what sort of a shock?

Frieda sat with a grim face, thinking of the ridiculous fuss there had been when Oliver left. Children swarming all over him, stuffing things into his pockets; a three-legged mongrel that should have been shot, jumping up and down—and all of them running after the taxi and waving like lunatics.

Between Fulton and Frieda sat Oliver, holding his presents carefully on his lap. A flashlight from Trevor, a box of crayons from Nonie . . . they must have saved up all their pocket money. There was a huge "Good Luck" card, too, signed by everyone in the home. Even Sparky had added her paw mark in splodgy ink.

The taxi was crawling, caught in a jam. Now it stopped for a traffic light ahead. Looking out of the window, Fulton saw a number of signs on a tall gray house.

ADOPT-A-GHOST, said one . . . DIAL-A-GHOST, said another.

Dial-a-ghost? Now where had he seen those words before? Of course, on the leaflet he'd picked off the mat at Helton when he went ahead to give orders to the servants. *Every kind of ghost,* the leaflet had offered. . . .

Fulton bared his yellow teeth in the nearest he ever came to a smile, and his eyes glittered.

He knew now what he was going to do.

. Chapter 5 .

N O SOONER HAD Oliver's taxi disappeared down a side street than two nuns, looking like kind and intelligent penguins in their black-and-white habits, made their way up the steps of the agency. It was one of the days when people came to ask for ghosts, not ghosts for people, and as soon as she saw them, Miss Pringle felt that something good was going to happen.

Mother Margaret, who was the head of the convent, came to the point at once.

"We have been very lucky," she said, "and our order has just moved into new buildings. Very beautiful buildings with a cloister and a refectory, and a little chapel where we shall be able to pray without the rain coming onto our heads from the broken roof."

"God has been very good to us," said Sister Phyllida.

"So we wanted to share our good fortune," said Mother Margaret.

"You see, our old abbey buildings are still standing. It was too expensive to pull them down and we thought we might offer a home to a suitable family. They would be quite undisturbed. We shouldn't trouble them . . . and of course we would expect them not to trouble us."

Miss Pringle was becoming very excited.

"You know, I think I have just the family for you. The nicest ghosts you could possibly ask for."

"I know you will understand that we need ghosts who are not too noisy. Sadness wouldn't worry us," said Mother Margaret, "or cold kisses from bloodstained lips. We would completely understand about sadness and cold kisses. Someone headless would be all right, too, as long as they didn't frighten the goats. We keep goats, you know."

"And bees," said Sister Phyllida eagerly. "It's quite a little paradise we have at Larchford Abbey. Our rose garden—"

"Yes, the bees are important. We ourselves would not be disturbed too much by screams and that kind of thing, but bees are very sensitive. So we would ask you to be very choosy."

"Indeed, yes—I think you couldn't help being pleased with the Wilkinsons. You wouldn't mind a very old lady? She has rather a fierce umbrella, but she is an excellent person and in no way shriveled or withered—or at any rate, no more than is usual at her age."

"Being shriveled or withered would be no problem at all," said Mother Margaret with her kind smile. "We are used to nursing old people and have great respect for them."

"Then there is Mr. Wilkinson—he was a dentist, a most upstanding man, and his wife is one of the nicest people you could imagine. She has done wonders trying to make the knicker shop into a home."

Miss Pringle blushed, wondering if she should have said the word "knicker" in front of nuns, but they did not mind in the least.

"They sound just the sort of people we want," said Mother Margaret. "And I may say that the accommodation we offer must be what any ghost would want. A ruined cellar—rat-infested of course. A roofless chapel, overgrown with weeds, that is the nesting place of large white owls. A tumbledown refectory with a fireplace open to the roof . . ."

"And such a pretty bell tower," put in Sister Phyllida, "full of tangled ropes and iron rings and trapdoors. A child would love to play there." She looked wistfully at Miss Pringle. "There don't happen to be any children?"

"But there are, there are! Eric is a teenager and a bit wrapped up in himself, and there's a delightful little girl— she's not a real Wilkinson, they found her lost and abandoned, but they quite think of her as their own. She's rather strong-willed and very fond of animals but—"

Miss Pringle paused, wondering if she should warn the nuns about Addie's passion for unusual pets. But the nuns just said that it was natural for children to grow up with animals, and it was arranged that the family should come to Larchford Abbey in three weeks' time.

"Friday the thirteenth seems a nice date," said Mother Margaret, looking at her diary. "Ghosts would like to come on a date like that, I feel sure."

"Yes indeed," said Miss Pringle, quite overjoyed at the news she was going to give the Wilkinsons. "Now, if you would just be kind enough to fill in this form . . ."

• • •

That night in the Dirty Duck the ladies had not one port and lemon, but two.

"If only we could get your Shriekers placed as happily," said Miss Pringle.

Mrs. Mannering sighed. "I don't know what's going to become of them, Nellie. They're wrecking the meat store, and that servant of theirs has climbed into one of the containers and passed out cold. I keep wondering what would happen if someone came for a tray of hamburgers and found a completely frozen ghoul."

Miss Pringle made sympathetic tutting noises. "We must just go on hoping, dear," she said. "Perhaps getting the Wilkinsons fixed up will turn our luck."

. Chapter 6 .

I S THIS REALLY MINE? All of it?" asked Oliver.
"Yes, it is," said Fulton grimly. "I hope you're
impressed."

But Oliver was not impressed; he was appalled. They
had driven through a spiked iron gate along a gravel
drive and now stood at the bottom of a flight of steps on
either side of which were statues. To the left of Oliver
was a lion being stepped on by a man who was beating
him on the head with a club. On the right was an even
bulgier man wearing a sort of diaper and strangling a
snake. The windows of the tall gray building stared like
a row of dead eyes; unnecessary towers and battlements
sprouted from the roof, and the front door was studded
with nails.

Almost worse than the gloomy building and the
statues of animals being bullied by bulging men was the
icy wind sighing and soughing in from the sea. Tall
trees bent their branches; rooks flew upward, shrieking.

Everything at Helton looked gray and miserable and cold.

Oliver shivered and wondered again if there was some way he could give the place away. Perhaps he should ask his guardian? Colonel Mersham sounded sensible, trying to save the lemurs in the rain forest and looking for golden toads—but he wasn't going to be back for months.

The door now opened from the inside and Oliver found himself in a stone hall that was full of things for killing people: crossed pikes, a blunderbuss, a row of rusty swords fastened to the wall . . . A stuffed leopard snarled from a glass case, and beside it stood the butler and the housekeeper waiting to greet him.

Oliver thought he had never seen two people who looked so old. The housekeeper, Miss Match, had a gray bun of hair and a pink hearing aid stuck lopsidedly to one ear. The butler, Mr. Tusker, was bent almost double with rheumatism. As Oliver shook their dry leathery hands, he was shocked that they should be working as servants; they should have had servants working for them.

"Dinner is ready in the dining room, sir," said Miss Match to Fulton. She had been told to take her orders from him and she was too ancient and tired to be curious about the little boy who now owned Helton Hall.

Oliver followed them down a long corridor hung with portraits of the Snodde-Brittles in heavy golden frames. They passed through a shuttered billiard room . . .

a library with rows of leather-bound books locked up behind an iron grille . . . and reached the dining room, where Oliver's first meal at Helton Hall was waiting.

It was a meal he never forgot. Cousin Fulton and Cousin Frieda made him sit at the head of the table, and his feet, hanging down from the high carved chair, didn't even touch the ground. The table was the size of a skating rink, the room was freezing cold—and beside his plate were more knives and forks than Oliver had ever seen in his life.

"Start from the outside in," Matron had told them when they went for a treat to the Holiday Inn and had a proper banquet. So he picked up the round spoon and ate the soup, and then Mr. Tusker shuffled away and came back with a very red-looking bird and some potatoes and cabbage. Oliver ate the vegetables and took two mouthfuls of the bird, which was full of round dark pellets and tasted of blood. Then he put down his knife and fork.

"Have you finished, sir?" asked the butler.

"Yes, thank you," said Oliver.

"What's the matter, boy?" said Fulton. "There's nothing wrong with the meat, is there?"

"No, I expect it's fine, but I don't eat meat. I'm a vegetarian."

"A vegetarian?" said Fulton, his eyes bulging.

"A *vegetarian?*" echoed Frieda.

"A lot of us were in the Home. About half. It was after we saw a film about a slaughterhouse."

No one said anything after that. It was as though Oliver had said he was a wife-beater or had the plague.

But if the meal was bad, going to bed was much, much worse.

"You're to sleep in the master bedroom," said Frieda. "It's up in the tower, quite on its own. Nobody will bother you there."

"I don't mind being bothered," said Oliver in a small voice. "Couldn't I sleep a bit closer to other people?"

"Certainly not," said Fulton, for it was part of his plan to keep Oliver as lonely and as far away from help as possible. "The owner of Helton has always slept in the tower."

So Oliver followed Cousin Frieda up a wooden staircase, through the Long Gallery with its faceless statues and rusty suits of armor, along a corridor lined with grinning African masks ... up another flight of steps—a curving stone one this time, lit only by narrow slits in the walls—down a second corridor hung with snarling heads of shot animals . . . and reached at last a heavy oaken door.

The room in which he found himself was huge; the single light in its heavy shade scarcely reached the corners. Three full-length tapestries hung on the wall. One showed a man stuck full of arrows; one was of a deer having its throat cut; and the third was a battle scene in which rearing horses brought their hooves down on screaming men. An oak chest shaped like a coffin stood by the window, and the bed was a four-poster hung with dusty velvet curtains and the words *I Set My Foot Upon My Enemies* carved into the wood.

"The bathroom's through there," said Frieda, opening a door beside the wardrobe. "I'll leave you to unpack and put yourself to bed."

Oliver listened to her steps dying away and followed her in his mind along the corridor with the stuffed heads, down the curving stone stairs, through the corridor of masks, across the Long Gallery. . . . He had never in his life felt so alone.

The bathroom was a room for giants. All the cupboards were too high for him, and the only way he could reach the lavatory chain was to stand on the seat. In the bathtub, scrubbing himself with a long-handled brush that hurt his skin, Oliver tried hard not to think about the Home. Bath time had been one of the best times of the day; they'd blown bubbles and told silly jokes and afterward there was cocoa and a story from Matron. They were reading *The Lion, the Witch and the Wardrobe.*

The only way to get into bed was to run fast across

the bloodred carpet and leap in under the covers. But it didn't help much. He could still hear the stealthy *tap-tap* of the tassel of the blind against the window—and surely there was *something* in that big brown wardrobe . . . the way it creaked even when there was no one near.

The sound of footsteps returned. At the thought that someone had come back to say good night to him, Oliver brightened and sat up in bed. Perhaps they did care at Helton; perhaps he wasn't quite alone.

Cousin Frieda entered the room.

"Well, you're all settled, I see." She moved to the bed and looked down at the inhaler that Oliver had put on the night table beside him. "You won't want that," she said briskly. "I'll put it in the bathroom cabinet."

"Oh no, please." Oliver was frightened now. "I always have it by my bed. Sometimes I need it in the night."

"Well, it won't be far away," said Frieda. She took it off to the bathroom and put it in the high medicine cupboard, far out of Oliver's reach. "Now, I know you're not one of those silly children who ask for night-lights," she said, and her bony fingers moved toward the switch.

She was halfway out the door when Oliver's choked voice came out of the darkness. "Cousin Frieda," he said. "There aren't . . . are there any ghosts here? Does Helton have ghosts?"

Frieda smiled. Standing in the shadows in her black dress, she might have been a phantom herself.

"Really, Oliver," she said. "What a silly question! Of *course* there are ghosts in a house as old as this."

Then she shut the door and left him alone in the dark.

. . .

Fulton was in the drawing room, smoking a cigar.

"It'll work, Fulton, you're right," said Frieda. "He's scared already—in a week or two he'll be ready."

Fulton nodded. "I've had another look at the leaflet, and there shouldn't be any trouble about getting what we want. 'Spooks of every kind,' it says. I'll ring up in the morning to make an appointment. I'll go down in a few days and book some that'll do the trick. Then, when the boy's properly softened up, we'll move them in."

"You hadn't thought of us being in the house when . . . you know. Not that I'm frightened in the least, but . . ."

"No, no. When the time's right we'll go away and leave him quite alone. I tell you, Frieda, our troubles are over. Helton is as good as ours!"

. Chapter 7 .

THREE DAYS LATER Fulton walked into the
Dial-a-Ghost Agency. He had put on a blond
wig and gave his name as Mr. Boyd because he
didn't want anyone to know what he was doing to
Oliver.

Mrs. Mannering smiled at him. "What can I do for
you, Mr. Boyd?" she asked.

"Actually, it's more what I can do for you," he said.
"Which is to offer a home to some ghosts. But not any
ghosts. I want fearful ghosts, frightful and dangerous
ghosts. Ghosts that can turn people's limbs to jelly."

Mrs. Mannering leaned forward eagerly. Was it possible that she could get rid of the Shriekers at last?

"You see, I think that people nowadays want a bit of
danger," Fulton said. "They want a thrill. They don't
want things to be boring and tame."

"No, no, of course not. You are so *right!*" cried Mrs.
Mannering. "If only more people thought like you!"

"Now, I'm the manager of this big house in the north of England. It's been empty for a long time and now the owners want to open it to the public. They want to charge money for letting people go round the place."

"Yes, I see. It's sad the way these stately-home owners have fallen on hard times."

"Only of course there's a lot of competition in this business. At Lingley they've got lions and at Abbeyford they've got a funfair and at Tavenham they've got a boating lake. Well, there's nothing like that at the place I'm talking about. So I thought if we got some proper ghosts we could advertise it as 'The Most Haunted House in Britain' or 'Spook Abbey' or some such thing. That should pull in the crowds."

"It should indeed," agreed Mrs. Mannering. "Only I have to ask . . . what would you offer the ghosts—and what would you expect from them?"

"What would we *offer* them? My dear Mrs. Mannering, we'd offer them accommodation like no ghosts in Britain could boast of. Thirteen bedrooms with wall hangings. Corridors with howling drafts and hidden doors. Suits of armor to swoop out of . . . and a master bedroom with a coffin chest which they could have entirely to themselves. As for what we'd expect—well, some really high-class haunting. Something that would make people faint and scream and come back for more."

Mrs. Mannering was getting more and more excited.

"My dear Mr. Boyd, I have exactly the ghosts for you! Sir Pelham and Lady Sabrina de Bone. They come from a very good family, as you can gather, and would be absolutely at home in such a setting."

"They're the real thing, are they? You know . . . icy hands, strangling people, rappings, smotherings?"

"Yes, indeed. All that and more. Pythons, bloodstains, nose stumps . . . I promise you won't be disappointed. There's a servant, too, who I believe is very fiendish, but he's in cold storage at the moment, so I haven't seen him. There's only one thing—the de Bones really hate children. Especially children asleep in their beds. Of course, if the house is empty at night that wouldn't be a problem. But I would be worried about any children going round the house with their parents."

"We would certainly have to be careful about that," said Fulton smarmily. "I tell you what, we could put up a notice saying 'This guided tour is not suitable for children under twelve.' Like in the cinema. We might even build a playground so that the children are kept out of the way."

"That sounds fine," said Mrs. Mannering. "Quite excellent. Now tell me, how soon would you like them to come?"

Fulton was silent, thinking. Oliver was already going under, but he needed a bit longer to get properly softened up. "How about Friday the thirteenth," he said. His lips parted over his yellow teeth and Mrs. Mannering realized he was smiling. "But I have to make it quite clear that I won't take anything namby-pamby. You know, spooks wringing their hands and feeling guilty because they stole tuppence from the Poor Box or were nasty to their mummy. I need ghosts with gumption; I need evil and darkness and sin."

"You will get them, Mr. Boyd, I promise you," said Mrs. Mannering.

As soon as her visitor had gone, Mrs. Mannering hurried across the corridor and hugged her friend. "You were right, Nellie, our luck has turned! I've found a place for the Shriekers!"

"Oh my dear, what wonderful news! When are they leaving?"

"Friday the thirteenth—the same day as the Wilkinsons!"

The following morning they each wrote out the adoption papers, and made careful maps for both sets of ghosts and instructions about what to do when they arrived at their new homes. They put the Wilkinsons' maps into a green folder and the Shriekers' maps into a red folder and placed them in the filing cabinet, ready for the day when the ghosts would leave.

"Now be sure and look after these very carefully," they told Ted, the office boy, who was to give the folders to the ghosts.

And Ted said he would. He was a nice boy and a hard

worker, but he had a secret that he had not told the ladies. It was a small secret, but it was about to change the destinies of ghost and human alike.

. . .

Oliver had been at Helton ten days and no one would have recognized him as the cheerful, busy child he had been in the Home. He was pale, his dark eyes had rings under them; he jumped at sudden noise.

He knew he had to be grateful to Cousin Fulton and Cousin Frieda, who had come to stay with him even though the boys at their school needed them so much, and he knew that people couldn't help how they looked.

But he couldn't feel comfortable with them, and there was no one else to talk to. The servants were so old and deaf that it was a wonder they didn't drop down dead every time they picked up a duster, and the people who worked outside weren't friendly at all. The gardener hurried away whenever he saw Oliver, and the people from the village scarcely spoke to him.

Oliver did not know that Fulton had told them to avoid the young heir.

"The boy's delicate," he told everyone. "He's got to be kept absolutely quiet."

So Oliver spent most of the day alone, which was exactly what Fulton had planned. He wandered down the long corridors, being sneered at by the Snodde-

Brittle ancestors in their heavy frames. He sat in the library turning over the pages of dusty books with no pictures in them, or tried to pick out tunes on the piano in the dark drawing room, with its shrouded windows and enormous chairs.

If the inside of Helton was gloomy and dank, the outside was hardly any better. The weather was windy and gray, and the garden seemed to grow mostly stones: stone statues, stone benches covered in rook droppings, stone fountains with cracked rims. The lake was a black, silent hole, and something bad had happened there.

"A stupid farmer drowned himself," said Frieda.

"Oh!" Oliver looked down into the water, wondering what it was like to lie there in all that blackness. "Is he still there?"

"I expect so," said Frieda. "It was his own fault. He had the cheek to fall in love with a Snodde-Brittle."

"Didn't she want him?" Oliver asked.

"*Want* him? A Snodde-Brittle *want* a common farmer! Don't be stupid, boy."

Something bad had happened on the hill behind the house as well. Two hikers had been caught in a blizzard and frozen to death.

"They were townies," said Fulton. "Not properly dressed."

"I'm a townie, too," said Oliver. "I come from a town."

But he could see that it was the fault of the hikers for

freezing, just as it was the fault of the farmer for falling in love.

What made everything so much worse for Oliver was knowing that all his friends in the Home had forgotten him.

"We'll write to you at *once,*" Nonie had promised. "Even before you get there we'll start."

Everybody had said they would write straightaway, and Matron, too.

But they hadn't. Every day he waited for a letter and every day there was nothing at all. Oliver had written the very first morning, trying not to sound miserable and drawing them a picture of the Hall. Since then he'd written three more letters and he hadn't had a single one back, not even a postcard.

"Are you *sure,* Cousin Fulton?" Oliver said each day as Fulton returned from the post office, shaking his head.

"Quite sure," Fulton would say. "There was nothing for you. Nothing at all."

And Oliver said no more. How could a boy brought up to trust people as he had been look into the black heart of a man like Fulton? How could he guess that the letters he wrote to his friends were torn up before they ever reached the post office, and that the letters that came for him—lots of letters and postcards and a little packet from Matron—were destroyed by Fulton on the way back to the Hall.

Even thinking that Fulton might have made a mistake and not looked properly made Oliver feel guilty, because his cousin was trying so hard to be kind. Every evening, for example, Fulton would take him into the drawing room and turn out the overhead light and tell him ghost stories.

"You like ghost stories, I'm sure," Fulton would say, making Oliver sit beside him on the sofa. "All the boys in my school love a good, creepy story and I bet you do, too."

Then he would start. There was the story of the eyeless phantom who tapped each night on the windowpane asking to be let in, and when the window was opened, he seized the person and sank his teeth into their flesh. There was the story of the wailing nun who plucked off people's bedclothes and strangled them as they slept, and the story of the skeleton who came to look for his own skull.

"And do you know where he found it?" Fulton would say, bringing his face close up to Oliver's. "In an old coffin chest exactly like the one in your room!"

Then he would pat Oliver on the head and Frieda would come and say, "Bedtime, Oliver!" and the little boy would go alone through the Long Gallery with its faceless marble statues, along the corridor lined with grinning masks, up the cold stone staircase, past the bared teeth of shot animals . . . and reach, at last, his room.

Oliver did not cry; he did not run back and beg to be allowed to stay downstairs. But as he lay in the cave he had made for himself under the bedclothes, he thought he wouldn't mind too much if it was over soon; if they came quickly, the ghosts who were going to get him. If he was frightened to death he could go and lie quietly under the ground in the churchyard. He had seen the graves and the tombstones covered with moss, and it had looked peaceful there.

And for a child to think like that is not good at all.

. Chapter 8 .

IN THE KNICKER SHOP, the Wilkinsons were having a party. It was the day before they were due to leave for their new home in the country and they had invited their friends to say good-bye. Mr. Hofmann had come from the bunion shop, sniffing a little because he was going to lose Grandma. A lovely Swedish phantom called Pernilla, with luminous hair and gentle eyes, had drifted in from the music store. There was a jogger who had jogged once too often, and various children Addie had picked up: the son of a rat-catcher who came with a dozen of his father's phantom rats, and a pickpocket called Jake who knew everything there was to know about living off the land.

It was a good party. Though the ghosts were sad to see such a nice family leave the district, they tried hard not to begrudge the Wilkinsons their good luck.

"Ahhh . . . imagine . . . to breathe again the fresh clean

air," sighed Pernilla, who was dreadfully homesick for the pine forests of her native land.

"And living with nuns," said the jogger, who had been a curate before he dropped dead of a heart attack on the jogging path. "Such good people!"

Aunt Maud was everywhere, filling glasses with her nightshade cordial, making people feel comfortable.

"If only you could all come with us," she sighed.

"Maybe you can," said Adopta. "If the nuns are so kind, maybe they'll make room for you all!"

She had filled Grandma's gas mask case with the ghosts of beetles and wood lice that she meant to resettle in the country, and was so excited that she found it impossible to keep still.

Everyone had been very well behaved up to then, but perhaps Aunt Maud's drinks were stronger than she real-ized, because Eric, who was usually so quiet, suddenly said, "No more knickers!" and sent a box of mini-briefs tumbling to the floor.

"No more Tootsies and Footsies and Bootsies," shouted Grandma, who had been particularly annoyed at the silly names that people nowadays gave to socks, thwacking at the display stand with her umbrella.

"And down with tummy buttons," yelled Adopta, and a pile of polka-dot bikinis tumbled from their shelves.

At first Aunt Maud and Uncle Henry tried to stop

them, but it was no use. The relief of getting away from all that underwear was just too great, and soon even Mr. Hofmann, who could hardly glide, was thumping a see-through nightdress with his crutch, while Pernilla zoomed to the ceiling with a box of body stockings that she draped like streamers round the lamp.

But when the clock struck eleven, they quieted down. Mr. Hofmann was led away by Grandma, the jogger jogged back to his path, the rat-catcher's son called to his rats . . . and the host and hostess, as is the way with parties, were left to clean up the mess.

There was only one more thing to do. Sober and solemn now, the Wilkinsons filed out into the street and called to Trixie.

"We love you, Trixie," they said, bowing to the north.

"We need you, Trixie," they said, bowing to the east and the west and the south.

"And we shall never forget you," they promised.

Of course, if Trixie had come just then, it would have been a miracle, but she didn't. So they went back to pack and cover the budgie's cage, while Uncle Henry made his way to the Dial-a-Ghost Agency and the office of Miss Pringle.

The folder with all their instructions and the maps was exactly where the office boy had said it would be, on the windowsill beside the potted geranium. Uncle Henry took it and passed it backward and forward across his chest so as to cover it with ectoplasm and make it invisible.

And an hour later, the Wilkinsons were on their way.

• • •

The Shriekers did not have a farewell party. To have a party you need friends, and the Shriekers didn't have any. All the same, in their dark and nasty way they were excited.

"A place that's fit for us at last," said Sabrina. "Statues . . . suits of armor . . . a tower!"

Mrs. Mannering had come herself to tell the Shriekers about Helton Hall, which was noble of her, because the frozen meat store had not been a nice place even before the de Bones came, and now it was unspeakable. Sides of beef lay sprawled on the floor where the ghosts had tried to drink blood from them; sheep's kidneys and gobbets of fat squelched underfoot.

"Perhaps there'll be some children we can scare to death," said Sir Pelham, and the hatred in his eyes was terrible to see.

"A little girl I can scratch with my fingernails," Sabrina gloated. "Long, deep scratches right to the bone."

"A little boy I can squeeze and squeeze till he turns blue and chokes."

But now it was time to thaw out the ghoul and get ready to leave. They had tipped him out of his container the night before, but he was still rigid, and while Sir Pelham beat him with his riding crop, Sabrina jerked the rope round his neck and screamed her orders. "You're to get up, you pullulating blob. You're to get up and cook something and clean something and pack something and hurry!"

While the poor ghoul tottered about muttering, "Fry! Sizzle! Sweep!" Sabrina made herself beautiful for the journey. She squeezed the juice from a pig's gallbladder and dabbed it behind her ears, she smeared her dress with lard to give a shine to the bloodstains, and she unknotted the python from her neck and fed him a dead mouse.

Meanwhile, Sir Pelham glided to the Dial-a-Ghost Agency and through the window of Mrs. Mannering's office. The folder with the maps in it was just where Mrs. Mannering had promised. It even had *de Bone* on it in Ted's rather wiggly handwriting.

And as midnight struck, the de Bones, too, dragging their wretched servant by his rope, set off for their new life.

• • •

Oliver had woken with the feeling that he just couldn't go on. He would have run back to the Home, but the letter he wrote to Matron, begging her to let him return, had gone unanswered like all his other letters.

So there was nowhere to go. He got up wearily and

dressed and began the long journey down to the dining room, where Fulton and Frieda were waiting.

"We have a nice surprise for you, Oliver," said Frieda. "You've been looking a bit pale lately, so we've asked Mr. Tusker to drive you to the sea. He's going to York tonight to visit his sick sister, so this is your last chance to see something of the countryside."

Oliver felt guilty, of course. He'd thought how creepy Frieda and Fulton were and here they were planning a treat. The idea of seeing the sea cheered him up. They'd gone to the seaside a few times from the Home. There'd been donkey rides and ice cream and he and Trevor and Nonie had made the best sandcastle on the beach.

But when doddery Mr. Tusker stopped the car beside the dunes, Oliver realized he'd been silly again. The sea at Helton wasn't at all like that. The butler wouldn't even get out of the car. He handed Oliver a packet of sandwiches. "Don't come back till four. We're to stay out till then," he said as he shut all the windows and unfolded his newspaper.

So Oliver trudged off across the tussocky grass and tumbled down onto the shore. The wind hit him so hard he could scarcely stand upright; the waves slapped and pounded and thumped; dark clouds raced across the sky. The tide was high, so there were no rock pools, and as he fought his way up the beach, he was almost blinded by flying sand. After a while he gave up the struggle and climbed into a hollow between two dunes, where he ate his sandwiches. Then he dug a deep hole and lay down in it and fell asleep.

It was teatime when they got back to Helton. Mr. Tusker drove off to the station, and Oliver made his way to the dining room. A glass of milk and some biscuits were laid out on the table, but there was no sign of Fulton and Frieda. Instead, beside his plate, there was a note.

Dear Oliver,

I'm afraid we have had to go away for a few days. The boys in our school have been unhappy without us, and there has been some trouble which we have to put right. I know you will not mind being alone. After all, the master of Helton Hall has got to get used to being by himself. Miss Match has left your supper on the kitchen table; it is her day off and she is going to spend the night in the village, but there is plenty of food in the larder. We will be back as soon as possible.

Your affectionate
Cousin Fulton

Oliver looked up, straight into the sinister marble face of the god Pan, crouching on top of a clock. It was true, then. In all the thirty rooms of Helton, he was the only living soul.

I won't panic, he told himself. *I'll manage.* He drank his milk and went outside. It was less frightening out of doors, but no more cheerful. He walked round the dark lake with its drowned farmer, through the grove of weeping ash trees, up the hill where the two hikers had died . . .

The cold drove him in at seven, and he went to fetch his supper. The kitchens were down in the basement. He made his way through the maze of dank stone corridors, sure that at every corner something was waiting to pounce . . . past a pantry where dead birds hung by their legs . . . past an iron boiler chuntering like an evil giant . . .

The kitchen was huge, with a scrubbed wooden table. On the table was a tray with a salad, slices of bread and butter, and a glass of lemonade. He ate there, and, when he had finished, carried his empty dishes to the sink. It was then that he noticed the calendar hanging on the wall. It was a pretty calendar with views of the countryside, and the day's date circled by Miss Match.

Friday the thirteenth. The unluckiest day of the year! The day that ghosts and ghouls and vampires like best of all!

At that moment Oliver knew that it would happen this very night—the thing he waited for every time he crawled into the great bed and pulled the covers over his head. It might be the flesh-eating phantom at the window, it might be the wailing nun who strangled people with their sheets, or the skeleton looking for his skull . . . but one of them would come.

And when they did, he would die.

. Chapter 9 .

THE WILKINSONS TRAVELED by train.

The 1:00 A.M. from King's Cross Station goes direct to York, where you must be sure to leave the train, said the instructions in the folder.

So the Wilkinsons, who were all invisible of course, settled themselves down and had a very pleasant journey. The one o'clock was a sleeper, the kind with cubicles and bunk beds, and people were already lying in them, but the ghosts were used to making do. Grandma stretched out on the luggage rack, Addie and Eric lay down on the floor, and Uncle Henry and Aunt Maud took the budgie to the deserted dining car.

Traveling by train is always enjoyable, and when you don't have to pay fares there is an extra glow, but Uncle Henry, as the train raced through the night, was troubled. He was so sure that Miss Pringle had said the nuns lived in the West Country, and there was no doubt that York was in the north. Several times he checked the instructions in the folder, but what they said was perfectly clear.

"I must be getting forgetful," he said worriedly. "It's a good job I'm not a dentist anymore. I'd be pulling out the wrong teeth."

At York they got out, stretching their limbs in the cold dawn, and made their way to the station buffet.

Your next train, which leaves from Platform Three, is the 11:40 for Rothwick. You must, however, get out at Freshford Junction, which is the fifth station after York.

"Well, nothing could be plainer than that," said Henry. "And yet I was sure Miss Pringle said that the nuns lived in the west. I remember her mentioning the gentle climate."

"It certainly isn't very gentle here," said Aunt Maud, for a fierce draft was whistling in at the door of the refreshment room.

They decided to say nothing to the others for fear of worrying them, and punctual to the minute, the 11:40 drew up at Platform Three.

The next part of the journey was slow and the scenery wild and beautiful. They traveled through heather-clad hills and valleys with brown rushing rivers and little copses of wind-tossed trees. Both the children, as they looked out of the window, were lost in dreams. Eric imagined himself camping alone by a stream, his tent perfectly pitched, his kettle hissing over the fire, which he had lit with a single match, as Scouts learn to do. He would be whittling a stick with his lethal knife and there she would be, Cynthia Harbottle herself, stumbling into his camp, soaked to the skin and terrified.

"Eric," she would say, "Eric, I am lost, save me, help me, and I promise I will never look at an American soldier again."

Addie's dreams were different. She was watching the hillsides covered with shaggy, black-faced sheep. Surely in a place where there were so many of these animals, just one would pass on and become a ghost? She had always wanted a phantom sheep; she was absolutely sure she could train it to sit, or even to fetch a ball she threw for it. Sheep were much cleverer than people realized. They had to be, or Jesus would not have preached about them so much.

Grandma's thoughts were in the past. She was worried about Mr. Hofmann in the bunion shop. He was such a clever man, a German professor who had been a teacher at the university before he fell into the canal from thinking about poetry instead of looking where he was going. But he was not very strong-minded. Every time he woke and saw a picture of a stomach, he got a tummy ache, and every time he saw an enamel bowl, he wanted to cough into it, and he was working himself into a dreadful pother.

I shouldn't have left him, thought Grandma.

At Freshford Junction, the last part of their journey began.

You must now take the bus to Troughton-in-the-Wold, which leaves from the first stand opposite the station. Go to the terminus at a pub called the Horse and Hounds, cross the road, and make your way along the lane that leads uphill between clumps of firs.

Once again, everything went like clockwork. They found the lane and glided along it in the fading light. Then suddenly their way was blocked.

Uncle Henry opened the folder once more.

After a mile, you will find yourself in front of a high gate with griffons on the pillars. When you reach that, your journey is over.

"This is it, then," he said. "No doubt about it. This is the place."

It was a shock. Their new home was not at all what they had expected. Jagged battlements glowed black against a crimson sunset, writhing statues led up to the great front door . . . and the griffons' claws rested on a shield with the words *I Set My Foot Upon My Enemies* carved into the stone.

Grandma was the first to speak.

"I won't curtsy," she said. "Let's get that clear. It may be grand but I won't curtsy to nobody."

She had been very poor when she was young, and was forced to work as a housemaid in a big house, and it had made her very cross with anyone who was a snob and ordered people about.

"No, of course not, Grandma," said Maud. "Whoever heard of a curtsying ghost?" But she herself was very troubled. "Henry, are you sure it's us they want? I mean . . . shouldn't we be more . . . you know . . . skeletal and headless? Won't they expect hollow rappings and muffled moans . . . and that sort of thing?"

"You can moan through my muffler, Ma," said Eric. But he was only trying for a joke. The little scarves that Scouts wear round their necks are not at all suitable for moaning through.

The only person who wasn't in the least put out was Adopta.

"I can't see what the fuss is about," she said. "It's just a house with roofs and windows like any other." And as she spoke, Aunt Maud wondered yet again what Addie's life had been before she came to them.

But Uncle Henry now read out the last of the instructions.

You are asked to wait till midnight and then go to the master bedroom in the East Tower and begin your haunting. Good luck and best wishes for your new life.

"Come on, then," said Addie. "What are we waiting for?" And before they could stop her, she had swooped up the gravel drive and zoomed into the house.

. . .

Oliver did not think he would be able to sleep, but he did sleep—a restless, twitchy sleep filled with hideous dreams.

Then suddenly he was awake. The clock in the tower was striking, but there was no need to count. He knew it was midnight. He knew by the frantic beating of his heart, by the shivers of terror running up and down his spine, and by the clamminess of his skin.

He tried to sit up, and felt the familiar tightening of his chest. He was going to have an asthma attack . . . and he reached for the inhaler before he realized it was gone.

And then, as he was struggling for air, he saw it. A hand! A pale hand coming through the wardrobe door, its fingers searching and turning . . . The hand was attached to an arm in a white sleeve: a wan and lightless limb, sinister and ghastly.

The wailing nun? The murdered bride?

The other arm was coming through now . . . and dangling from it on a kind of string was something round and horrible and loose.

Its head. The phantom was carrying its head.

Knowing that his end had come gave Oliver a sudden spurt of strength. Managing to draw air through his lungs, he sat bolt upright and switched on the light. "Come out of there," he called, "and show yourself."

The figure did as it was told. If it was a nun or a bride, it was a very small one, and it seemed to be dressed for bed.

"Who are you?" asked Oliver, between the chattering of his teeth.

The ghost came forward. "I'm Adopta Wilkinson," she said. "There's no problem about *that*. But who are you, because you're certainly not a nun."

Oliver stared at her. She seemed to be about his own age, with a lot of hair and sticking-out ears. "Why should I be a nun?" he asked. "It's you who are supposed to be a nun. And headless."

"Do I *look* headless?" she asked, sounding cross.

"No. I thought . . . your sponge bag was your head."

The ghost thought this was funny. "Would you like to see what's inside?" she asked.

Oliver nodded and she unpacked her tooth-cleaning things. Then she took out the fish and put it down on the bedspread, where it lay looking peaceful, but not at all energetic. "I tried to find a friend for him when we were living in the knicker shop. I haunted every fish-monger in London—you know how there are always rows and rows of dead fish on the slabs—but not one of them had become a ghost to keep him company. Not a single one."

"He doesn't look unhappy," said Oliver.

"No." Addie repacked her bag. "But I don't understand; we were supposed to come to a convent, and this can't possibly be a convent. Nuns don't have little boys, and they wouldn't have those awful rude words carved everywhere." She pointed to the head of the bed and the words *I Set My Foot Upon My Enemies* carved into the wood.

"No, that's the motto of the Snodde-Brittles," said Oliver.

"They sound awful. I bet the feet they set upon their enemies have yellow toes with hair on them and bunions."

Oliver began to explain about Helton, but he was interrupted by the most extraordinary sound: a gurgling, guggling sort of noise ending in a hiccup.

"Good heavens, what's that?"

"Don't worry, it's only Aunt Maud. She's practicing wailing woefully or moaning muffledly—you can't be sure. She's terribly worried, you see, about not being dreadful enough for you. All of them are. Shall I tell them it's all right?"

"Yes, please do. And Adopta, could you just make it clear that muffled moans are not at all big with me?"

So one by one the Wilkinsons came and Addie introduced them. As soon as she saw Oliver, all the nonsense about being horrible went straight out of Aunt Maud's head and she glided over to the bed and gave him a big hug. Being hugged by a ghost who cares about you is a most wonderful feeling, like resting inside a slightly bouncy cloud. Not since he had left the Home had Oliver been so comfortable.

"Well, this is a big room for a small boy," said Aunt Maud. "And I can't see the point of all those nasty people hanging on the wall, but never mind . . . we'll soon have you shipshape."

Grandma then came down from the curtain rod where she had been hovering.

"I said I wouldn't curtsy," she said, "and I mean it. But the dust up there's shocking, and if you find me a nice feather mop in the morning, I'll give it a good going-over."

Eric had been standing by the door. Going to new places always made him shy and brought out his old worries about his spots and being unhappily in love, but now he came forward and gave the Scout salute, and then the budgie fluttered his wings and said, "Open wide," and "My name is Billie," and even "Ottle," which was the nearest he could get to saying Cynthia Harbottle, this not being an easy thing for budgerigars to say.

But Uncle Henry now took charge. "I think we should make ourselves known to your parents. It would be polite and they might have orders for us."

"I don't have any parents," said Oliver. "I'm an orphan. I lived in a home till three weeks ago and they brought me here. I'm . . . I'm actually . . . I mean, I seem to *own* this place," he said, and blushed because it really embarrassed him, having this huge house when so many people had nowhere to live.

The ghosts stared at him in amazement. This small boy who had welcomed them so warmly was the owner of Helton Hall!

"Well, in that case, we had better speak to your guardian or whoever is in charge of you."

"There's no one here, Uncle Henry." Calling this manly ghost "uncle" made him feel less alone in the world. "I've got some cousins but they're away, and so are the servants. There's no one here at all except me."

Aunt Maud couldn't believe her ears. "You mean you're all alone in this great barracks of a house?"

Oliver nodded. "Actually," he said, "I was a bit frightened before you came. But now . . ." He looked up and gave her the most trusting and delightful smile.

"Well, that's it, then, isn't it?" said Grandma. "We wanted something to do and we've got it." She gave Oliver a prod with her umbrella. "I can tell you this, little sprogget, while there's a spook called Wilkinson left on this planet, you aren't going to be alone again."

• • •

An hour later, the ghosts were settled for sleep. Grandma was in the coffin chest, Eric was curled up on top of the wardrobe, and Uncle Henry and Aunt Maud lay side by side on the hearth rug.

As for Addie, she'd made it perfectly clear where *she* was going to spend the night.

"That bed is far too big for you," she said to Oliver. "We'll lie head to feet and if you snore I'll kick you."

It was when she came back from cleaning her teeth that Oliver noticed a dark patch on her arm where the sleeve of her nightdress had rolled back.

"Have you hurt yourself?" he asked.

She shook her head. "You mean that mark on my ectoplasm? It's a birthmark. I've always had it."

"Goodness! They have them in fairy stories and then people come and say: 'You must be my long-lost daughter, the Princess of So-and-So!'"

Addie was not pleased. "No one had better try any of that stuff on me. I'm a Wilkinson and that's the end of it."

Her eyes began to close, but she forced them open. "Oliver, when we came here we passed a farm right close to your grounds. Does that belong to Helton, too?"

"Yes."

"Well, look ... if ... just *if* there happened to be a sheep who'd passed on ... you'd let me have it, wouldn't you?"

"Of course I would. You shouldn't even *ask*," said Oliver. "And anyway—"

But at that moment Aunt Maud's cross voice came

from the hearth rug. "Will you two stop talking at *once* and go to sleep."

Oliver smiled. Matron had sounded just like that when they were fooling around in the dormitory. Feeling wonderfully safe, he closed his eyes, and for the first time since he'd come to Helton, he fell into a deep and dreamless sleep.

. Chapter 10 .

THE NUNS OF Larchford Abbey were very excited. It was the morning of Saturday the fourteenth and they knew that their ghosts had come. The owls had screeched horribly, the field mice had scuttled for shelter, and the bell in the ruined chapel had given a single, deathlike clang. Moreover, when they woke at dawn they saw that a strange, chill vapor hung over the old buildings that they had offered to their guests.

"Oh, it is a real adventure, having proper spooks!" Mother Margaret said.

"Yes, indeed. What is better than being able to share our lovely home with others," said Sister Phyllida.

Larchford Abbey was certainly a most beautiful place. Set in a green valley with a little burbling stream, it was surrounded by gardens and orchards. Bees flew up from the hives, the apple trees were coming into blossom, and a herd of pedigree goats gamboled in the meadow.

"I wonder if we shouldn't just go and see if they have

settled in all right," said Mother Margaret in her kind and caring way. "We wouldn't bother them, of course, but there may be some little thing they would like to make them comfortable."

"Yes indeed," said Sister Phyllida, who had been a nurse before she became a nun and was very practical and sensible. "The first few days in a new place are so important."

They waited till the evening and then made their way over the wooden bridge that led to the ruined part of the Abbey.

"We must remember that this is their breakfast time; they will only just have woken up. Sometimes people are not very friendly first thing in the morning."

"Oh dear, I hope they're not in bed," said Mother Margaret. She remembered that there had been a gentleman, a Mr. Wilkinson, and it had been a long time since she had seen a gentleman in bed.

When they had crossed the stream, they saw, on the path leading to the door of the ruined building, a set of footprints. They were truly horrid footprints, made by a specter with only three toes, and they stopped suddenly, as though the ghost who made them had got bored with walking and had suddenly become airborne.

"Oh, isn't this thrilling!" said Mother Margaret, clapping her hands.

"I wonder what happened to the other two toes?"

said Sister Phyllida. Nurses are interested in that kind of thing.

Before they reached the door of the Abbey, they had another treat.

"Look, Sister—bloodstains. I'm sure they are." Mother Margaret bent down and dipped her finger in the red pool, and sure enough her finger came away with a sticky dark spot.

"They must have settled in," said Sister Phyllida. "People don't make bloodstains, I'm sure, unless they feel at home."

But when they reached the door of the bell tower and pushed it open, the noises they heard did not seem to be those of a contented family of ghosts at breakfast.

The Shriekers were quarreling, as usual.

"And what exactly is that?" Sabrina yelled at her husband, throwing something soft and furry at his face.

"It's a dead shrew, you loathsome grub-pot," screeched her husband.

"Oh, ha, ha, you've frightened it to death I suppose! Why don't you frighten something your own size? Don't lie to me. That shrew has been dead for days. It stinks."

"Of course it stinks. And you stink, too. You've got rotten egg yolk oozing out of your ear hole."

"I should just hope I do stink. I swore I would stink from the day of our Great Sorrow. I swore I would stink and suffer and claw and kill!"

Fortunately, the nuns down below could not hear the actual words that the Shriekers were saying. They did, however, get the idea that their new guests were not completely happy and relaxed.

"Of course it's often like that with married people before breakfast," said Mother Margaret, who knew that a lot of couples are best not spoken to before they have had their early morning cup of tea.

"And the journey may have been a strain," said Sister Phyllida. "Larchford is rather low-lying; it takes time to get used to the damp."

So the kind nuns decided they would leave their new guests to settle in, and call again on the following day. "Though I would have loved to see the little girl. She sounded like such a dear thing in her nightdress with her sponge bag and the fish."

When the nuns had gone, the Shriekers went on quarreling and pelting each other with foul things they had found on the floor of the ruined abbey. Then suddenly they got bored and decided they were hungry.

The ghoul lay on a tombstone, quivering in his sleep.

"Wake up and cook something, stenchbag!" screeched Lady de Bone, twitching his rope.

"And be quick about it or we'll nail you up by your nostrils," yelled Pelham.

As they screamed at their servant and jerked his rope,

the ghoul became madder and madder, uttering his weird cooking cries and waving his frying pan to and fro.

"Fry!" he gabbled. "Sizzle! Burn!"

As he ran about, the pan became less gray, more reddish . . . hotter. Suddenly it burst into flame, and he scooped a dead owl from a rafter, tore its feathers off, and threw it into the fire. Then he tossed two burned thighs at the de Bones and collapsed again onto the slab.

Back in the convent, the smell of cooking came quite clearly to the Sisters.

"That's their breakfast now," said Mother Margaret. "They'll soon feel better."

"There's nothing like a nice cooked breakfast to settle the stomach," agreed Sister Phyllida. "So many families just start the day with nothing but a piece of toast, and it's so unwise."

They felt very relieved, sure now that the ghosts they had invited were going to lead a sensible life, and then they said good night to each other and went to bed.

But the Shriekers, tearing the flesh off the roasted owl, were not exactly being sensible. Mind you, they had had a very difficult journey. The mouse had not agreed with the python, who had been sick, and the ghoul kept passing out at the end of his rope and had to be dragged like a log. And when they had at last lost height and come down where the instructions had told them to, they had seen none of the things they had been prom-ised. No great hall with towers and battlements, no writhing statues, no suits of armor or stone pillars or iron gates. Instead there were a few tumbledown buildings and a ruined abbey with the most awful feel to it—the feel of a place where people had been *good*.

And then when dawn broke they had seen something that made them stagger back in horror: a row of nuns on their way to the chapel to pray!

"I'm not staying here!" Sabrina yelled. "I'm not hav-ing that awful gooey goodness clogging up my pores. I can feel it between my teeth. Ugh!"

But they had been too tired to glide back at once. Now they decided to wait for a few days and gather up their strength.

"There might be a child we can harm," said Pelham.

"How could there be? Nuns don't have children."

"No. But they might run a school."

The idea of scratching and strangling and smother-ing a whole school full of children cheered Sabrina up a little.

"Well, all right. But I won't stay for long."

"Don't worry," said Pelham. "I'm all set to make those women in the agency wish they'd never been born!"

. Chapter 11 .

A NEW AND HAPPY life now began for Oliver.
He woke to find Adopta sitting at the bottom
of his bed and heard the other ghosts splashing
about in the bathroom and thought how wonderful it
was not to be alone.

They all came down to breakfast and made themselves invisible while Miss Match brought him toast and
cereal. Just as she was putting it down, the budgie said,
"Open wide," and she jiggled her hearing aid and said,
"I'm not going to open wine at this time of day. Wine is
for supper."

"I'll bet she can't see us," said Adopta. And before
Aunt Maud could stop her, she flitted off into the
kitchen.

"I told you," she said when she came back. "I leaned
over her and said, 'Boo,' and she just went on reading
some silly story in the paper. We've got nothing to worry
about there."

But in any case, Miss Match was only supposed to leave out Oliver's meals. The rest of the day she spent in the village with her cousin. Fulton's plan to leave Oliver quite alone was turning out to be the best thing that could have happened.

The ghosts simply loved the house.

"Oh, my dear boy," said Aunt Maud. "These cellars . . . the fungus . . . the damp! It's a bit strong for me, but just think what poor Mr. Hofmann would make of this place. How happy he would be!"

"Who's Mr. Hofmann?" Oliver wanted to know.

"He's Grandma's boyfriend," said Adopta. "He lives in a bunion shop and he's got every ghost disease in the book, but he's terribly clever."

The ghosts liked the kitchens and they liked the drawing room with its claw-footed chairs, and the faceless statues in the library. They liked the hall with its huge fireplace, which you could look up into and see the sky, and they absolutely loved the library with its rows of moldering books.

"I bet there are ghost bookworms in those books," said Adopta. "I bet they're *full* of them. Can I look later?"

"Of course. I wish you wouldn't *ask*, Adopta." Oliver sounded quite cross. "If Helton's mine, then what's mine is yours and that's the end of the matter."

If they liked the house, the ghosts liked the gardens even more. The weeping ash tree with its drooping branches, the rook droppings on the stone benches, the yew trees cut into gloomy shapes . . .

"It's so romantic, dear boy, so calm!" said Aunt Maud. "You can't imagine what it is like to be here after the knicker shop."

When they reached the lake, they found Eric staring down into the water.

"There is someone in there," he said. "Someone like me. Someone who has suffered."

"There's supposed to be a drowned farmer," said Oliver. He had been afraid of the body trapped in the mud, but already the ghosts were making him think of things differently.

Eric nodded. "He died for love," he said. "I can tell because of Cynthia Harbottle. She wouldn't go out with me even after I'd bought her a box of licorice allsorts. It took all my sweet ration and she didn't even say thank you. And this man's just the same. People who have been hurt by women can recognize each other."

"Can you call him up, dear?" said Aunt Maud. She was thinking how nice it would be if Eric could talk to someone else about being unhappily in love. When he talked to *her* about Cynthia Harbottle, she got terribly cross. Mothers always get cross when people do not love their sons, and Cynthia had been a nasty piece of work, wiggling her behind at American soldiers and smearing herself with lipstick.

"He doesn't want to, not now," said Eric. And Oliver couldn't help being glad. He didn't feel quite ready yet for a drowned farmer covered in mud.

But the farmer reminded Aunt Maud of something she wanted to ask Oliver.

"Now, please tell me honestly," she said, taking his hand. "Don't be polite. But . . . how would you feel if . . . if someone came here, someone *appeared,* who was only wearing a flag? Would she be welcome?"

Oliver was quite hurt that she should ask such a question. "Of *course* she would be welcome. Of course. A ghost wrapped in a flag would be . . . inspiring."

After lunch—which was a sandwich for Oliver in the garden—the other ghosts said they would rest, and Oliver and Adopta climbed up the hill to look at the place where the two hikers had frozen to death.

"I can't *feel* them," said Adopta. "I'm afraid they may just not have become ghosts. Perhaps it's as well if they had bad frostbite. But I think you ought to ask your factor to put up a proper cross or a little monument. It seems rude not to have anything."

"I don't know if I've got a factor. What is it exactly?"

"It's a person who runs an estate and tells the shepherds and farmers what to do."

"How do you know about factors? I mean you wouldn't have had them in the knicker shop or at Resthaven."

Adopta shrugged. "Sometimes I know things and I don't know how I know them, but please don't start on again about how I'm really someone else because I'm a Wilkinson and I'm me." She glanced round at the wide view, the heather-covered hills, the river. "Pernilla would love this. She feels so trapped in the shopping arcade."

"Who's Pernilla?"

"She's a Swedish ghost. She came to look after some children and learn English, and some idiot in a Jaguar drove her home from a party and crashed."

"Why don't you ask her to stay? And Mr. Hofmann, too. Anyone you want—there's lots of room here."

"Could we? Oh Oliver, that would be great. Only we'd better do it properly through the agency or—" She broke off and pointed excitedly at a field below them. "Look! Sheep! Hundreds of them. Come on!"

But when they reached the field, every single sheep in it looked fleecy and cheerful and well.

"I could kill one for you, I suppose," said Oliver. "But I don't eat mutton and—"

"No, that would be silly. It might not become a ghost and then it would be a complete waste of time. You can never tell, you see. You can get half a dozen animals that just lie there dead as dodos and absolutely nothing happens, and then one suddenly rises up, and you're off!"

The day ended with a great honor for Oliver. He was invited to the Evening Calling for Trixie. They did it near the sundial and everybody linked hands and bowed to the north and the south and the east and the west, and told Trixie that they wanted her and needed her and would she please, please come.

When it was over, Oliver asked if there was anything that Trixie had particularly liked.

"Something that we could put out for her, perhaps?" he said.

Grandma and Aunt Maud looked at each other. "Bananas," said Grandma. "She'd have sold her soul for a banana. All of us would in the war."

So Oliver ran back into the house and fetched a banana—a long and very yellow one—which they put on the sundial, where it could be seen easily from above, and Aunt Maud was so happy that she rose into the air and did the dance that she and Trixie had done when they were Sugar Puffs—a thing she hadn't done for years.

Oliver fairly skipped along the corridor that night on his way to bed, and when he got to his room he had a surprise. While he was out with Adopta, the others had redecorated his room. The man stuck full of arrows was gone, and so was the deer having its throat cut, and the rearing horses. Instead Aunt Maud had brought in some dried grasses and put them in a vase, and they'd hung up a cheerful picture of a garden they'd found in one of the other rooms.

And Oliver's inhaler was once again beside his bed.

"You won't need it," said Uncle Henry. "The air here is excellent, and anyway, asthma's something you grow out of. But it might as well be there."

Although ghosts usually haunt by night and sleep by day, they had decided to keep the same hours as Oliver. When everyone had settled down, Oliver still sat up in bed with his arms round his knees.

"What are you thinking about?" asked Adopta sleepily.

"I was thinking about how much there is to find out. About ghosts and ectoplasm and why some people become them and others not, and why some people see them and others don't . . . I mean, if you eat carrots you're supposed to see better in the dark, so perhaps there's a sort of carrot for making you see ghosts? And if you really knew about ectoplasm, maybe you could change the things that ghosts are wearing. I bet it's the flag that's bothering your aunt Trixie. Imagine if you called her and she could immediately put on a raincoat or a dressing gown. And wouldn't it be marvelous if people could *decide* whether to become ghosts or not."

"And decide for their pets," said Addie. It was always the animals that mattered to her.

Oliver nodded. "I tell you, someone ought to start a proper research institute to study all this."

"Not one of those places where they try to find out

whether we exist or not. Ghost hunting and all that. Tying black thread over the staircase and taping up the windows. So rude."

"No. This would be ghosts and people working side by side."

Oliver's mind was racing. He hadn't wanted Helton; he was going to try to give it away. But now ... Why not a research institute here? There was room enough.

"I wonder if I've got any money?" he said. "I mean serious money, for labs and people to work in them."

"Why don't you write to your guardian? He seems a nice man, exploring places and trying to find the golden toads. I expect the lawyer's got his address."

Oliver thought this was a good idea, but thinking about letters made him remember the one thing that still troubled him.

"What's the matter?" asked Addie, seeing the change in his face.

Oliver shrugged. "It's silly to fuss when everything's turning out so well, but I had these friends in the Home ..."

He explained what had happened and Addie frowned. "Was it always Fulton who posted the letters for you?"

"Yes. He used to take everything down to Helton Post Office. He said it would be safer."

"Hmm." Addie had never liked the sound of Fulton.

"Why don't you try once more when you write to your guardian and we'll take the letters to the box at Troughton?"

Oliver nodded. "Yes," he said. "That sounds sensible. That's what we'll do."

. Chapter 12 .

T HE GHOSTS WHOM the kind nuns had adopted had been at Larchford Abbey for several days, and the nuns were just a little bit disappointed and hurt. They knew that people needed time to settle into a new place, and they had made it clear to the ladies at the agency that they wouldn't bother the ghosts and that they didn't expect the ghosts to bother them.

All the same, a little friendliness would have been nice. They had looked forward to a glimpse of the child in her nightdress, playing merrily in the bell tower, or the old lady floating about in the rose garden, and having heard that Mr. Wilkinson was fond of fishing, they had half expected to see him by the river, casting with a rod or landing a trout with his net.

But there had been absolutely no sign of the family. Not one wisp of ectoplasm in the orchard, not a trace of a voice singing to itself in the dusk.

The ghosts were *there,* all right. Oh yes, they were definitely there. Blood had oozed through the old abbey floor, and they had found several sets of footprints with three toes. From time to time, too, there came the smell of frying meat—rather *strong* meat, which did not seem to be absolutely fresh—and now and again they heard a gurgling moan, but no one had come forward to introduce themselves or to thank the nuns for giving them a home.

"One must do good without thinking of the reward. One should not need to be thanked," said Mother Margaret.

"Do you think we ought to write to the agency?" asked Sister Phyllida. "I mean, there may be some little thing they are too shy to mention. Something we could put right?"

But Mother Margaret thought they had better wait a bit longer. "After all, we don't know very much about . . . ectoplasm and that sort of thing. Perhaps there are changes when people travel, which have to right themselves."

"Like airsickness. Upset stomachs and so on. Yes, that could explain a lot. Some of those bloodstains do look a little disordered," said Sister Phyllida, who was the one who had been a nurse.

It wasn't just the Shriekers' bloodstains that were out of order. The Shriekers themselves were in a ghastly state. They were lying on the floor and kicking the air with their moldering feet, and every time they thrust their legs out, they bellowed and whooped and howled and squealed.

They had remembered that it was the anniversary of their Great Sorrow. On an April day just like this one, the terrible thing had happened that had driven them mad with guilt and turned them into the ghastly, tortured, and revolting creatures they now were.

"Oi! Oi! Oi!" moaned Sabrina. "How could we have done it? How could we have been so cruel to our flesh and blood?"

"It is right to punish," whined Pelham. "People must be punished for doing wrong."

"But not like that. Whipping would have been all right, taking food away would have been all right. Thumping and scourging and walloping would have been all right, but not what we did."

She began to moan again and roll about on the floor among the owl droppings and scrabble her feet in the filth. Even as she did that, the guilt and sin made her little toe go all wibbly, and Pelham slapped her hard on the behind and said, "Stop it! I, too, suffer. I, too, feel my guilt and my sin, but you have hardly any toes left and enough is enough. We must act. We must be revenged on the world. We must see that no other child is left un-harmed to remind us of that ghastly day when our—"

"No!" shrieked Sabrina. "Don't mention that name. Don't dig the knife deeper into my bosom."

"You haven't *got* a bosom anymore," said Pelham. "It's all skin and bone and—"

They began quarreling again about whether or not Sabrina had a bosom. Then they sat up and tried to pull themselves together.

"It's true that we have to rid the world of children," said Pelham. "It's not till the sobs and moans of other parents mingle with our own that we shall get some rest. But there don't seem to be any children here, and in the meantime . . ."

He glided over to the window and stood looking out at the fields and stables and orchards that the nuns had tended so lovingly.

"In the meantime what?"

Pelham's scarred face was a grimace of hatred. "Meanwhile there are little lambs *gamboling*—" He spat out the word. "And puppy dogs playing . . . and baby goats—ugh—leaping for joy."

Sabrina came to join him. "Yes," she said. "And you know what they call baby goats. They call them *kids*. . . ."

. Chapter 13 .

"BEND OVER," said Fulton Snodde-Brittle, and
the small boy standing in front of him in his
study bent over.

"All the way over," said Fulton, and the child doubled
up over the arm of the leather chair. His name was Toby
Benson and he was just seven years old.

Fulton went for his cane, and then frowned and put
it back. Canes left marks and the school inspector was
due in the next couple of weeks. Not that it mattered.
By then he and Frieda should be living in Helton Hall
and the school could go to the devil. Still, might as well
play it safe. He fetched his gym shoe out of the cupboard
and bent it back. You could get quite a decent thwack
with that, but it wasn't the same. Everything had become
namby-pamby nowadays.

"You know why I'm going to beat you, don't you?"
said Fulton.

Toby sniffed and a tear ran down one cheek. "Yes, sir. Because I was eating sweets in the gym, sir. My mother sent me—"

"That's enough," roared Fulton, raising his arm.

But when he had finished, and the little boy had hobbled out, Fulton didn't feel as cheered as he usually did after beating a child. His mind was on Helton Hall and what was happening there. Oliver had been alone now for nearly a week and he had hoped to hear that the boy had been taken ill or gone off his head. Perhaps they should phone and find out what was happening? He went down to find Frieda, who was in the school kitchen telling the cook to remove one fish finger from every one of the children's helpings laid out for lunch.

"But that'll just leave one, Miss Snodde-Brittle," said the cook. "One fish finger's not much for a growing boy."

"Are you telling *me* what growing boys should eat?" said Frieda, towering over the poor cook. "You don't seem to be aware that overeating is very bad for children. It makes them fat and gives them heart disease. Now let me see you take the extra finger away and put it in the freezer for next week. And I thought I said *one* tablespoon of tinned peas." She bent over a plate and began to count. "I find it very hard to believe that twenty-three peas make up one tablespoon. I do hope you can count because—"

But at this moment Fulton appeared by her side and said he wanted to speak to her.

"I'm going to telephone Miss Match," he said, when they were alone in the study.

So he dialed the Helton number, and after a very long time Miss Match's voice could be heard at the other end. She had forgotten her hearing aid, and her voice sounded croaky and cross.

"Helton Hall."

"Ah, Miss Match. It's Fulton Snodde-Brittle here. I'm just ringing up to find out how Oliver is. How has he been?"

There was a pause at the other end. Then: "I've never given him any beans. It's the wrong time of year for beans. Beans come later."

Fulton tried again.

"No, not beans to eat. I want to know how he's getting on. Have you any news?"

"No, of course I haven't got any newts. Can't abide the things—slimy little nasties."

Frieda reached for the phone. "Let me try," she said. "I've got a more carrying voice." She put the mouthpiece to her lips. *"We want to know how Oliver is,"* she shrieked. *"How is he in himself?"*

There was another pause. Then Miss Match said, "Barmy. Off his head."

A great smile spread over Frieda's face.

"Barmy?" she repeated. "You mean mad?"

"Mad as a hatter," said the housekeeper. "Talks to himself, runs about waving his arms, won't come in for meals."

"Oh, that's wonderful—I mean that's terrible. But don't worry, Miss Match. We'll be back soon to take him off your hands."

She put the phone down and the Snodde-Brittles stood and grinned at each other. "It's worked," said Fulton. "Oh glory—think of it. Helton Hall is ours! We'll give him another three or four days to go off the deep end completely, and then we'll get a doctor and have him put away."

Frieda flopped down in the armchair. The thought of owning Helton was so marvelous that she almost thought of telling the cook to leave the second fish finger on the children's plates. But in the end she decided against it. Happiness didn't have to make you stupid.

. Chapter 14 .

WHEN THE WILKINSONS had been with Oliver for a week, they called up the ghost of the farmer from the lake.

Oliver had been worried about this, but it turned out to be a very good thing to do. They called him up the way they called Trixie, telling him he was wanted and needed and that he should not wander alone in the Land of the Shades, and gradually there was a sort of heaving on the lake, and then a kind of juddering, and slowly the spirit of Benjamin Jenkins, who had run the Home Farm at Helton a hundred years ago, floated up out of the water.

He couldn't have been nicer. He was simply dressed, in breeches and a checked shirt, and carried a gun over his shoulder because he had meant to shoot himself if the drowning didn't work, and the first thing he did in his pleasant country voice was to thank them for calling him up.

"I was getting a bit bogged down in there," he said, "but I couldn't make up my mind about coming out."

Eric and Mr. Jenkins took to each other at once, and in no time at all they were telling each other how badly they had been treated by the women they loved.

"Her name was Frederica Snodde-Brittle," said the farmer. "She used to ride through my fields every morning on a huge horse, and I was always there, holding open the gate for her. I was so sure she'd come to care for me."

"That's what I thought about Cynthia Harbottle. I used to carry her satchel all the way to the bus stop."

The farmer sighed. "She was so *haughty*. She said no Snodde-Brittle could marry a common farmer."

Eric nodded understandingly. "Cynthia was haughty, too. She used to blow bubble gum in my face."

Frederica hadn't done that, because bubble gum wasn't invented in those days and anyway the Snodde-Brittles were too haughty to chew, but she had done other things, and soon Eric and Mr. Jenkins took to wandering away into the woods, each one feeling very much comforted to know that he was not alone.

With Eric so much more cheerful, his parents could settle down to enjoy themselves. Uncle Henry went fishing, borrowing a rod from the lumber room and sitting peacefully by the river for hours on end. He didn't catch any fish—he didn't want to—he just liked to sit and be quiet and forget all those years when people had opened their mouths and showed him their teeth even on a Monday morning. And if anyone came and saw a rod stretched by itself over the water, they probably thought it was the branch of a tree.

Aunt Maud, meanwhile, took up her dancing again, hitching up her long tweed skirt and twirling and swirling on the rim of the fountain, and Grandma did housework. Miss Match never came upstairs, so that no one noticed a Hoover snaking along the floor by itself or a feather duster shaking itself out. Even the budgie became a useful bird, helping the swallows build their nests and hardly saying anything silly at all.

There was only one thing that puzzled the ghosts. Why had Miss Pringle not told them that they were going to Helton instead of to the nuns? And who was it that had offered to have the ghosts at Helton in the first place? Who had gone to the agency and offered them a home?

"It must have been Fulton," said Oliver. "He kept telling me ghost stories, but I didn't understand. I feel awful now, not liking him, when he was doing this marvelous thing for me."

The Wilkinsons looked at each other. They weren't so sure about Fulton Snodde-Brittle. Why had he left Oliver alone for days on end? And what had happened to the letters Oliver had given him to post? Because his friends in the Home had *not* forgotten him. There'd been an absolute spate of letters answering the one he'd sent from Troughton. They meant to keep a sharp eye on Fulton Snodde-Brittle when he came. And he came, as it happened, on the following day.

• • •

"I'm afraid you'll find the poor little boy in a dreadful state," said Fulton as he drove the car toward Helton Hall.

"Barmy," agreed Frieda. "Completely raving."

Dr. O'Hara said he was sorry to hear that. He was a young doctor with dark hair and a friendly smile, and not the doctor whom Fulton had hoped to bring to Helton. It was old Dr. Gridlestone whom the Snodde-Brittles had chosen to put Oliver away, but he was ill. Dr. O'Hara was new to the district and it was his day off, but when Fulton had told him that there was a child who might become a danger to himself and others, he had agreed to come.

"Is there any mental illness in the family?" Dr. O'Hara asked. "Any madness?"

"Is there *not!*" lied Fulton. "His mother thought she was a chicken and his aunt jumped off a cliff and his little sister had fits. Not the Snodde-Brittles, of course— the Snodde-Brittles are perfect—but the family on his mother's side."

"So you see how worried we are for Oliver," said Frieda. "He must be shut away somewhere and protected from the strain of running Helton Hall."

Dr. O'Hara was silent, wishing he hadn't come. The idea of picking up a struggling boy and carrying him off was not pleasant at all.

They turned into the drive and found Miss Match waiting for them.

"Well, how is the dear boy?" asked Fulton. "We've been so anxious about him, but Dr. O'Hara has come to examine him and we can get an ambulance in no time and take him away."

"Best thing you can do," said Miss Match grumpily. "He gets sillier and sillier."

"Is he in bed?"

"Not him. Rampaging round in the garden talking to himself. Won't come in for meals. Leaves bananas on the sundial."

Fulton and Frieda exchanged glances. "Bananas on the sundial, eh? That sounds serious, wouldn't you say, Dr. O'Hara?"

"It is certainly unusual," the doctor admitted.

"You'll find him by the lake," said Miss Match, and stumped back into the house.

So the Snodde-Brittles, followed by Dr. O'Hara, crossed the lawn and made their way down the gravel path toward the water.

Even from a distance they could see that Oliver was behaving very strangely. He was running round and round, beckoning and calling, and suddenly he burst out laughing.

"I think I'll just go back and see about the ambulance," said Frieda. She had remembered Fulton's description of the Shriekers, and even in broad daylight she didn't fancy meeting them.

But at that moment, Oliver looked up and saw them.

Fulton expected anything except what happened next. Oliver gave a shout of welcome and ran toward his cousin with his arms stretched out.

"Oh, thank you, *thank* you," he said, hugging him round the waist. "Thank you so much—so terribly much! I was so lonely and miserable and now everything's *lovely*!" He turned to Frieda, standing with her mouth open. "And Cousin Frieda, too! It's the best thing that's ever happened, you sending me the ghosts."

Fulton loosened Oliver's hands and took a step backward. He had left a pale, thin child whose eyes were too big for his face. Now he saw a boy with rosy cheeks and the glow that happiness brings. Was it a feverish flush? Yes, it had to be.

"What . . . ghosts?" he stammered. "I never sent any."

"Didn't you?" Oliver was puzzled. "That's strange. They said—"

"They? Who are they?" asked the doctor.

"Come and meet them. Please. They vanished when they heard the car because they thought they might be in the way." He took Fulton's hand and reluctantly the others followed. "Adopta's very excited because Mr. Jenkins has dredged up a phantom prawn for her and she thinks it might cheer up the fish in her sponge bag, but we're not sure because it's quite a *big* prawn."

Dr. O'Hara sighed. This was madness all right . . . and he'd really liked the little boy.

They had reached the lake.

"It's all right, everybody . . . please appear again," Oliver called. "It's Cousin Fulton and Cousin Frieda and—" He turned to the doctor. "I'm sorry, I'm afraid I don't know your name."

"I'm Dr. O'Hara."

"Oh, a doctor! Uncle Henry will like that. He was a dentist and he's a very scientific person. Good . . . there they are!" One by one the ghosts appeared and Oliver introduced them. "This is Aunt Maud . . . well, Mrs. Wilkinson, really, and this is Mr. Wilkinson, and this is Grandma . . ."

What followed kept Fulton and Frieda rooted to the ground. Dr. O'Hara stepped forward and shook hands with . . . nothing. With air.

"Pleased to meet you, Mrs. Wilkinson," he said. "And you, too, sir." He took another step and this time he raised his hand to his forehead in a salute. "I was a Scout, too," he said in his friendly way. "Though I never made it to patrol leader."

"Who are you talking to?" shrieked Frieda. *"What are you doing?"*

Dr. O'Hara turned to them, very surprised. "But surely you can see them?" he said. "This gentleman here in the army helmet and the old lady with the umbrella and—"

"No, we can't," said Fulton, white-faced. "You're making it up. You're playing a joke."

"No, he isn't, Cousin Fulton," said Oliver. "Those are the Wilkinsons. They're my family. Look, there's Adopta now—you *must* be able to see her. She's my special friend."

"Yes, you must surely see the little girl?" said Dr. O'Hara. "Her nightdress is quite dazzling."

"You're lying!" Fulton was shaking with anger and fear. He had brought in a doctor who was as crazy as the child.

Oliver was very upset. "Oh, how unfair, Cousin Fulton! That's really rotten, you not being able to see the ghosts when it was you who gave them a home."

But Addie didn't at all want to be seen by the Snodde-Brittles. She thought they looked horrible, with their long yellow faces and bulging eyes, and she was more certain than ever that Fulton was up to no good. Dr. O'Hara was another matter. And now the Snodde-

Brittles saw the doctor bend down and cup his hands as though something were being lowered into them.

"Ah yes—how interesting! I've never seen a phantom prawn before. I think you'd be quite safe putting her in with your fish. It's a female, and they only attack when they're laying eggs." He straightened himself and put his arm round Oliver. "You've certainly got a most delightful family," he said. "I haven't met such pleasant ghosts since I was a little boy in Ireland. Our house was haunted by such an interesting couple—a schoolteacher and his wife who drowned in a bog. They were the most wonderful storytellers." He walked over to Fulton and Frieda. "I can't see the slightest sign of mental illness in the boy; he seems as fit as a flea, and for someone who's going to run a place like this, an open mind about unusual things is most important. You must be so relieved to know that you have nothing at all to worry about."

But Fulton and Frieda had had enough. The last thing they saw as they hurried back to the car was a fishing rod lift itself into the air and drop into the doctor's hand.

"How very kind," they heard Dr. O'Hara say. "I must say an hour's fishing would be most pleasant. It so happens that it's my day off."

• • •

"It's your fault, you idiot," said Frieda when they were alone again. "You said you'd get ghosts that were going

to frighten him into fits, and look what you've done! Unless Dr. O'Hara's mad. Grandmothers. Boy Scouts. Little girls in nightgowns. It's ridiculous!"

"It's not my fault—it's the fault of that stupid woman in the agency. She swore she had a pair of spooks that would frighten the living daylights out of people. There must have been a mix-up, and I'm going to get to the bottom of it. I tell you Frieda, I'm not finished yet. I'm going to Set My Foot Upon My—"

"All right, all right," said Frieda grumpily.

She knew exactly where she wanted to put her own foot.

. Chapter 15 .

COLONEL MERSHAM SAT on a camp stool beside a meandering, dark brown river, reading a letter.

A turtle lumbered onto a sandbar, huge blue butterflies drank in the shallows, and in the rainwashed trees a family of howler monkeys caught each other's fleas, but the Colonel did not look up. He was completely absorbed in what he read.

"Interesting," he said. "An interesting boy and an interesting idea."

He was surprised. He had agreed to be Oliver's guardian because he was sorry for the orphaned boy, but he loathed the Snodde-Brittles, who had been his mother's cousins, and never went near Helton unless he had to.

This boy, though, was different.

He'd come upon a family of ghosts and a ghost child who cared with all her heart for ghostly animals, and he was asking for help. The boy had written:

I want to set up a research institute for the study of every-thing to do with ghostliness. I want to find out what ectoplasm is made of and what happens when people become ghosts—and animals, too. Addie is particularly worried about the animals: she says you can tell people what happened when they pass on, but you can't tell animals, and they get muddled and bewil-dered, and she'd like to make Helton into a safe place for them to be. Not a zoo, just somewhere they can live in peace.

Colonel Mersham put the letter down and looked upriver to where Manuel, the Spaniard who had helped him in his travels, had drawn up the canoe. They had journeyed two days and nights to the place where the fabled golden toads of Costa Rica had last been seen. They had searched every lily leaf, every clump of rushes, every stone, but they had come back empty-handed. The beautiful, palpitating, pop-eyed creatures, who had lit up the dark landscape like shimmering suns, were gone.

The Colonel had found it difficult to be brave about this. It was happening in so many places; marvelous ani-mals that lived on now only as memories: the aye-ayes of Madagascar, the tigers of Bali . . .

And now the golden toads. It had been his dream to see them ever since he was a boy.

Had he given up too early? he wondered. If he could not find a living toad, might he perhaps find . . . its ghost?

And if so, could it be brought back to Helton and cared for, so that people in the future would know what these marvelous creatures had been like?

The Colonel folded his letter and rose to his feet.

"Manuel!" he called to his friend. "Get the canoe ready! We're going back to search again!"

. Chapter 16 .

IT WAS THE worst day of their lives, both Miss Pringle and Mrs. Mannering were agreed on that.

When Mother Margaret and Sister Phyllida came into Miss Pringle's office, Miss Pringle was delighted. She liked the nuns enormously, and she hoped to get good news of her favorite family.

But one look at their faces and the question died in her throat. Mother Margaret looked as though she hadn't slept for a week; Sister Phyllida had obviously been crying.

"The most dreadful thing has happened," said Mother Margaret. "It has been the most terrible experience!"

"And frankly we don't understand how you came to do this to us, Miss Pringle. We only wanted to help."

Miss Pringle was growing more and more frantic. "But what *has* happened? Are you not satisfied with the Wilkinsons? Surely—"

"Satisfied!" Mother Margaret was no longer the kind and placid nun who had been to the agency before.

"*Satisfied!* When we have two lambs with dislocated legs and a kid with a gash in its throat still at the vet! When we nearly lost our favorite calf and the chickens will probably never lay again!"

"But I don't understand. What has gone wrong? Please explain. I sent you the nicest ghosts in—"

Mother Margaret rose from her chair. "The nicest ghosts! The *nicest!* I admit we are not worldly women, but you had no right to play such a trick on us. If nice ghosts swoop down on innocent animals and scratch them with their fingernails . . . If nice ghosts wear evil pythons round their throats and tear the feathers off baby chicks . . ."

She couldn't go on. Tears choked her.

"And the man, Miss Pringle!" Sister Phyllida took up the story. "That dreadful hoofmark, the vicious knees, the stench! He picked up a goat bodily and would have torn it limb from limb if Sister Felicity hadn't raised her crucifix. Not only that—poor Sister Bridget hit out at the lady with a rowan branch, and look!" She felt in the pocket of her habit and took out a small box, which she opened. "You can imagine how she felt when this dropped onto her head."

Miss Pringle leaned forward and her worst fears were confirmed. Quite clear to those who have an eye for such things was the decayed and bloodstained toe of Lady Sabrina de Bone.

She covered her face with her hands and moaned. "Oh

heavens, how terrible. It was a mistake . . . a ghastly, ghastly mistake. Our mistake, of course! We were asked for some really frightening ghosts for a stately home in the north and we sent the Shriekers. At least we thought we had. And you were supposed to get the Wilkinsons. I just can't understand it—we took such care to match you up." She, too, was almost in tears. "Thank goodness you knew about exorcism. I mean rowan twigs and prayers and so on."

"We *knew* about it," said Mother Margaret. "But it is not a thing we liked to do. We wanted to welcome lost souls, not banish them."

"Are they . . . the Shriekers completely . . . you know . . . destroyed?" asked Miss Pringle nervously.

"Not they! They just took off cursing and screaming, dragging that wretched blob along behind them. They were coming back to London, I believe."

Miss Pringle was beside herself. "You must let us make it up to you—the cost . . ."

But the nuns shook their heads. "There is no money that can make up to us for the terror and the sadness. Our new litter of puppies simply won't leave their mother at all. They spend their time *underneath* her—and the bees will take weeks to recover."

Though she was quite broken up by what had happened, Miss Pringle made a last plea for her favorite family. "You wouldn't consider trying the Wilkinsons instead? They—"

But she had gone too far. "Definitely not, Miss Pringle. Frankly, we are surprised that you can ask it," said Mother Margaret.

And leaving Lady de Bone's toe on Miss Pringle's desk, they went away.

When something bad has happened, what one needs more than anything is a kind friend to talk to. But when Miss Pringle hurried across the corridor, she found Mrs. Mannering as upset as she was herself.

"I was just coming over, Nellie. I've had that Mr. Boyd on the telephone—the one from Helton Hall. He was absolutely furious. It seems as though we sent him the Wilkinsons, and he wants them out. He says they're namby-pamby and useless and he wants the ones he ordered at once. He wants the Shriekers. But where are they?"

"I'll tell you where they are," said Miss Pringle.

When she had finished, Mrs. Mannering had turned quite pale. "The honor of our agency is at stake, Nellie. We must find out how it happened. I quite definitely put the Shriekers' maps in a red folder and gave them to Ted."

"And I quite definitely put the Wilkinsons' maps into a green folder and gave them to Ted."

So they went into the little office at the back where Ted was sorting out the mail.

"Now, Ted," said Mrs. Mannering, "there has been a

dreadful muddle, and we have sent the wrong ghosts to the wrong adopters. Do you remember my giving you a red folder to leave out for the Shriekers?"

"And do you remember my giving you a green folder to give to the Wilkinsons?"

Ted got to his feet and stood before them. He was blushing and looking very hangdog indeed.

"Yes, I do. But . . . Well, I left them out like you said . . . Only . . . you see . . ."

So then it all came out. He was color-blind. This didn't mean that he couldn't see *any* colors. He could see yellow and blue and violet perfectly well. But for a person who is color-blind, there is absolutely no difference between green and red. He had been afraid to tell them because he didn't want to lose his job.

"Oh Ted, you should have told us; it was very wrong of you. We wouldn't have dismissed you just for that, and now look at the harm you've done."

"We'll have to get a computer anyway," said Mrs. Mannering. "But in the meantime we must put this right at once. Fortunately, the Shriekers are still wanted at Helton, so I'll see if I can get hold of them and let them know."

"And I shall go to the Wilkinsons myself and break the bad news. The trouble is the nuns have been put right off adopting any more spooks, so we can't do a swop. You're sure they can't stay at Helton, too?"

"Quite sure. Mr. Boyd's really taken against them. He wants them out at once."

Miss Pringle dabbed her eyes. "It looks as though it's back to the knicker shop for that dear, nice family. You know, Dorothy, sometimes I think that life just isn't *fair*."

. Chapter 17 .

MISS PRINGLE ARRIVED at Helton late in the afternoon. Addie and Oliver were out for a walk, but Aunt Maud was waltzing about on the head of the man trying to strangle a snake, and she came down at once.

"Why if it isn't dear Miss Pringle," she said. "What a pleasure to see you. We should have let you know before how very happy and grateful we are."

Grandma, who was having a little nap on one of the benches, now sat up and said, "Yes, that's right. It's a lovely place here; we're as snug as anything. It just seems like a bad dream now, that time in the knicker shop." She called to Eric. "Eric, here's Miss Pringle from the agency come to see how we've settled in."

You can imagine how poor Miss Pringle felt. How she blushed and stammered and had to dash away her tears when she told them the dreadful news.

"A mistake?" said Uncle Henry, who had come to join them. "What sort of a mistake?"

Miss Pringle blew her nose and explained about Ted and the color-blindness.

"You were meant to go to some nuns down in the West Country. Ever such nice people. And some quite different ghosts were ordered for up here. Rather fierce and horrible people but . . . suitable for such a big place."

It was Uncle Henry who understood what she was trying to tell them.

"You mean you want us to leave here? To go away again?"

Miss Pringle nodded. "The gentleman who ordered the ghosts for here was very angry and upset."

The Wilkinsons could make no sense of this. All they knew was that they were not wanted.

"Of course we aren't headless," said Aunt Maud hopelessly.

"I told you," said Eric. "I told you no one would want me. If Cynthia Harbottle didn't want me, no one else will either."

"Now, Eric," said Grandma. He'd hardly mentioned Cynthia since they came to Helton and here it was starting up again. "It isn't you, it's me. It's because I'm old."

"No, no, no!" cried Miss Pringle. "It's just that Mr. Boyd wanted fierce ghosts and he's very cross. It's to do with attracting tourists."

But she looked round at Helton in a very puzzled way. There didn't seem to be any notices saying that the hall was open to the public.

Uncle Henry's ectoplasm had become quite curdled with shock, but he spoke with dignity. "If we're not wanted here, we must leave at once. Go and catch the budgie, Maud, and I'll get our things."

"Oh dear, oh dear!" Miss Pringle was getting more and more flustered. Still, she was running an agency; she had to be businesslike. "Where is Adopta?" she asked, for the little girl was a special favorite of hers.

"She's out with Oliver," said Aunt Maud, and when she thought of saying good-bye to the child they had grown to love so much, she could no longer hold back her tears.

"Oliver? Is that Mr. Boyd—the man who owns Helton?" asked Miss Pringle. "Because if so, perhaps I'd better stay and apologize to him myself."

But just then the children came running down the path. Oliver had found another letter from Trevor in the Troughton Post Office and his face was alight with happiness. At least it was till he saw the ghosts.

"What is it?" he asked, suddenly afraid. "What's happened?"

Miss Pringle came forward and introduced herself. "I'm afraid I've had to tell them that they aren't wanted here at Helton. That they were sent here by mistake."

The next minute, she stepped back a pace because the most extraordinary change had taken place in the little boy.

He had seemed to be a gentle sort of child and not at all bossy or strong-minded. Now his chin went up and his eyes blazed.

"Not welcome at Helton?" he said furiously. "Not *welcome!* How dare you say such a thing! They're the most welcome people I have ever known. They're my friends. They're my family and they're not going away from here ever. I'll . . . I'll kill anyone who tries to take them away."

The effect of Oliver's words was incredible. The ghosts' ectoplasm seemed to thicken and grow stronger. Grandma's whiskers, which had faded almost to nothingness, stood out clear and sharp again, and Eric smiled.

"Oh, you good, kind boy," said Aunt Maud, and came to put her arms round him.

Miss Pringle, though, was completely muddled.

"You see, dear, the man who owns this place—"

Oliver, usually so shy and never one to interrupt, broke in.

"*I* am the man who owns this place," he said, and it seemed quite reasonable that this little boy, who scarcely came up to Miss Pringle's shoulder, should talk of himself as a man. "I didn't want to but I do—you can ask anyone—and I hated it here till the Wilkinsons came, and *I will not let them go.*"

Miss Pringle stared at him. "But the person who came to the agency was a grown-up—a tall man with a long face and a mustache. And he said he wanted a very particular kind of ghost—"

"That wasn't the owner. That was my cousin, Fulton Snodde-Brittle, and it was very nice of him to order some ghosts because I was lonely. But whatever he ordered, these ghosts are *mine.*"

Miss Pringle had turned pale. She had just taken in what Oliver had said. "You mean you really own this place? And you live here all the time? You sleep here at night?"

"Yes."

Miss Pringle's hand flew to her mouth. Mrs. Mannering had found the Shriekers cursing and raging in the meat store and told them they could go to Helton.

And the Shriekers had sworn to destroy any child that they could find!

"Oh heavens!" said Miss Pringle. "How dreadful. Oh, whatever should I do?"

. Chapter 18 .

"A T LAST!" cried Sabrina de Bone. "At last a place that's fit for us!"

The Shriekers stood in the hall at Helton, looking about them with their greedy, hate-filled eyes. It had become very cold; a rain of soot came roaring down the chimney, and a dead jackdaw tumbled out onto the hearth.

In the dining room, the pictures of the Snodde-Brittles fell to the ground and lay in a mess of twisted string and broken glass. A suit of armor crashed onto its side.

"Nice," said Sabrina. She floated into the drawing room and drew her fingernails along the sofa . . . and the cloth ripped apart, letting the stuffing ooze out like clotted blood.

The hands of the clock began a mad whirring, and an icy mist crept along the floor.

"Something's going on," said Mr. Tusker, down in the basement. "Don't like the sound of it."

"Better go see if the boy's all right," said Miss Match.

But Mr. Tusker didn't think that was a good idea at all. "Not me," he said, and bolted the kitchen door.

The Shriekers floated on through the grand rooms, dragging the ghoul behind them. Blue flames sprang up in the fireplace and terrified mice scuttled deep into the wood paneling.

Then suddenly Sir Pelham stopped.

"Do you smell anything, snotbag?" he asked.

Sabrina's nose stump began to twitch. She turned her face this way and that.

"Oh yes, I smell something," she drawled. "I smell something . . . lovely."

Sir Pelham yanked the rope and the ghoul gurgled and choked.

"Where is it, you slime-gobbet?" he asked. *"Where is the child?"*

With his eyes still shut, the ghoul began to run wildly about. "Child," he muttered. "Burn. Fry. Sizzle. Child." He set off across the drawing room, through the billiard room, toward the staircase . . .

"The smell's getting stronger," said Sabrina happily. "And it's a *clean* child. A washed child. I do love hurting clean children."

"Clean children are the best," agreed Sir Pelham.

Dribbling with blood lust, they followed the ghoul as he panted up the staircase . . . across the Long Gallery . . . down the corridor with the grinning masks . . .

. . .

It was the crash of falling Snodde-Brittles that woke Aunt Maud.

"Is that you, Eric?" she called, for the farmer and Eric had decided to go camping in the woods.

But the noises that came from downstairs were not the kind made by her shy son. Squealings . . . rappings . . . and now the sound of a clock striking twelve . . . and thirteen . . . and on and on.

"Henry, I'm bit worried," she began.

But her husband was already sitting up, and now Grandma popped her head out of the coffin chest.

"There's some hanky-panky going on somewhere," she said. "I can tell by my whiskers. They're as stiff as boards."

"I'm going downstairs to see," said Uncle Henry. "You stay here."

But of course there was no way the women would let him go alone.

They did not have far to go before they saw the intruders. A pair of crazed, blood-spattered specters, and, pulling them along, a quivering blob of jelly with foaming jaws.

"Stop!" Uncle Henry spoke like the brave soldier he had been in the war. "This part of the house is private."

The female spook tittered. "You funny man," she said. She unwound the python from her neck, and it hissed and swayed and shot out its flickering tongue.

But the Wilkinsons stood their ground.

"You can't come any further," said Aunt Maud. "You'll wake the children."

Poor Maud . . . she realized almost at once that she had made a terrible mistake.

"Ah, *children*." Sir Pelham gloated. "Not just one child! One *each,* then. We won't have to share! I'm going to strangle mine."

"I'm going to cut mine to ribbons with my nails."

"No, you aren't!" Grandma stepped forward and lunged out with her umbrella. Uncle Henry plucked a sword from the wall. They were ready to fight to the last drop of their ectoplasm, but then something so horrible happened that they stopped just for a moment—and that moment was fatal.

The budgie, trusting and stupid, had followed them. Now he landed, fluttering and squawking, on Aunt Maud's shoulder.

"Open wide," said the bird in his friendly way. "Open—"

But it was the python who opened wide. And as the Wilkinsons stared in horror, watching their beloved pet

disappear into the jaws of the evil snake, the Shriekers passed through them as if they were morning mist and entered the room where the children lay fast asleep.

• • •

They lay head to feet as usual. Addie had become invisible. She always vanished when she slept.

The moon was full, and the quiet room was bathed in a silver light.

"Child," gabbled the ghoul, and collapsed in a heap on to the rug.

The Shriekers stepped over him and moved toward the bed.

"Ah, how sweet, a little boy in his pajamas," sighed Sabrina, and stretched out her fingers, with their dreadful nails, to touch his cheek.

And in that instant, Oliver awoke.

"Are you all right, Addie?" he asked sleepily. Then he fell back on the pillow, and the scream died in his throat. Bending over him was a specter so hideous that he couldn't have imagined it in his wildest dreams. She had no nose; her hollow eyes glittered with hatred; gobbets of raw meat clung to her hair.

It's impossible, he thought, *I can't be seeing this.*

Then he wondered if maybe it was a sort of joke. "Are you wearing a costume, Aunt Maud?" he managed to say.

But he knew it wasn't so. From the appalling spook there came such a sense of loathing and danger that no one could have pretended it. And now, looming up behind her, was a second specter even more gruesome: a man with a broken skull who raised the whip he held in his hand . . . and laughed.

"Well, well, you look a nice healthy fellow, all safe and sound in your bed. What a pity your last hour has come!"

But as the female phantom's fingers began to move toward his throat, something happened to Oliver that was far worse than anything the spooks could do. His chest tightened . . . his breath came in choking gasps . . . the air he had drawn into his lungs stayed trapped. Desperately, he stretched out his hand for his inhaler . . . he had almost reached it—and then the thong of the man's whip curled round it and dashed it to the ground. Even as the vile specters prepared to throttle him, Oliver was turning blue in the worst asthma attack of his life.

He tried to cry out and warn Addie, but there was no hope of making a single sound. *This is it, then,* thought Oliver. *This is the end.*

But Addie was awake. Without bothering to become visible, she went on the attack.

"How dare you?" she screamed. "How *dare* you harm Oliver, you disgusting old spooks." Kicking out at Pelham with one foot, she swooped down and picked up the inhaler. "Breathe!" she ordered Oliver, putting it into his hand. "Go on. *Do* it."

"Who are you? What's going on here?" spluttered Pelham, who could see nothing.

"What's going on here is that I'm going to do you in," yelled Adopta. "I don't know where you come from, but I'm not scared of you, you silly old banshees." She aimed a kick at the ghoul, lying on the floor, then swooped up to bite Sabrina in the neck. "If you've hurt Oliver, I'll kill you. I'll turn your ectoplasm into spaghetti; I'll grow maggots in your ear hole."

As she walloped and thumped and kicked, Addie was slowly becoming visible. Her nightdress was beginning to show up now, and her long hair.

"Well, go on," roared Pelham to his wife. "Do her in. Finish the little spitfire 'off. The boy's done for anyway."

But Lady de Bone was standing quite still. Her loathsome mouth hung open and she was staring and staring.

"What's the matter with you?" yelled Pelham to his wife. "What are you gawping at?"

"I feel . . . strange," said Sabrina.

Addie was moving in for the kill. She rose into the air, ready to punch the female phantom's nose stump into a pulp, and as she did so, she rolled up the sleeve of her nightdress.

And Lady de Bone screamed once . . . screamed twice . . . and fell in a dead faint on to the floor.

. Chapter 19 .

TOBY BENSON, the little boy whom Fulton had beaten so cruelly, sat on his suitcase in the hall at Sunnydell Preparatory School and smiled. His parents were coming to take him away forever, and he was so happy he thought he would burst.

The inspectors had been to the Snodde-Brittles' school and said it had to be closed at once. The teaching was a disgrace, they said, and Fulton was not fit to be a headmaster.

But if the boys had left, and the cook and the cleaning ladies and the sports master, there were other people who had come. The greengrocer who supplied the school with vegetables had come, waving his bill. The butcher had put a ladder against the house and stuck his head in at the bathroom window and told Fulton he'd turn him into a bowl of black pudding if he didn't pay what was owing. Even now, a van from the electricity company had drawn up and two men got out, ready to cut off supplies.

"We're going to end up in prison for debt if this goes on," said Frieda, looking down at the street.

"No, we aren't. We're going to end up in Helton Hall. We're going to own the farm and the grounds and the forest and have proper servants to wait on us."

"Well, I hope you're right. That horrible little boy seems to be spook-proof as far as I can see."

"He won't be spook-proof with this new lot. I tell you Frieda—" He broke off. "Good Lord, look who's here! It's Mr. Tusker getting out of a taxi."

Getting out of a taxi was not an easy thing for Mr. Tusker to do. He was too bent and his legs were too wobbly. But he managed it at last, and then they saw that Miss Match was in the taxi, too.

"This is it, Frieda. I just feel this is it."

It looked as though he was right. When the house-keeper and the butler reached Fulton's study, they were gray with shock. They had come to give notice. Mr. Tusker was on the way to his sister in York and Miss Match was going to stay with a niece in Scotland and neither of them was ever going to spend another minute in Helton Hall.

"We tried to tell Mr. Norman," said the butler. "But he's away and his secretary's a twitty little thing. So we came to let you know and to give back the keys." He laid a great bunch of labeled keys on the table. "We want you to sign that we've given them to you, and a month's wages is owing to us."

"Yes, yes. Mr. Norman will pay them when he returns. But why? Why are you going in such a hurry? What's happened at Helton?"

Mr. Tusker started to wheeze and Miss Match hit him on the back. "Everything. It's haunted. It's full of evil. Things fall."

"Things burn."

"There's a creeping mist in all the rooms."

"There's screams to make your hair stand on end."

"Oh dear, how terrible," said Fulton. "And the boy?"

"Gone!" said Mr. Tusker.

"Dead, it's my opinion," said Miss Match. "Drowned."

"Drowned! But how terrible! How ghastly!" Fulton's voice rose to a shriek. "Tell us more! Tell us more!"

"We found his clothes by the lake. Shoes. And a shirt floating on the water. And the lake looks . . . funny."

"But how appalling! The poor little boy. Have you told the police?"

"It's not our job to tell the police, Mr. Snodde-Brittle. We've given back the keys and you've got our notice. And a month's wages is owing—"

"Yes, yes. You shall have them of course. I'll tell Mr. Norman. Just leave your addresses."

• • •

"It's happened!" shouted Fulton when the butler and the housekeeper had left. "I told you! The woman in the agency said they were spooks to end all spooks. They've obviously frightened the boy into fits and he's run into the lake. I told you he wasn't stable."

"Yes, but even if he's dead, what are we going to do about the spooks? I'm not staying in the place with those nasties hanging round."

"Now, Frieda, why don't you trust me? I wouldn't have set all this up if I hadn't had a card up my sleeve."

"You mean exorcism and all that? Salt and rowan twigs and that sort of stuff? Because—"

"No. Nothing as feeble as that. It might work on those soppy Wilkinsons in their nightgowns, but it wouldn't work on the Shriekers. No, this is something different," said Fulton gloatingly. "This is *science*."

He opened a drawer and handed her a newspaper cutting, which she read carefully, and then read once again.

"I see," she said, licking her lips. "Yes. You don't think it will be expensive?"

"What does that matter? Once we have Helton we'll have all the money in the world. We can cut down the forests and sell the wood. We can bulldoze the farm for development properties—we'll be rolling."

"Yes." Frieda put down the newspaper and looked down at the street. Toby Benson was just running out to meet his parents. They were going to take him out to Africa with them rather than send him to another boarding school. "You don't think he'll . . . Oliver . . . he'll come up from the lake and haunt us?"

"For Pete's sake, Frieda, what's got into you?" He pushed the newspaper under her nose. "You can read, can't you? There isn't a spook on the planet we can't destroy with what they've got there."

"Yes." Fulton was right. It was silly to think of Oliver lying at the bottom of the deep dark pit that was Helton lake. No one got anywhere who let themselves get soft.

. Chapter 20 .

THE LETTERS ABOVE the grimy redbrick building said THE SAFEGUARD SEWING MACHINE COMPANY, but it wasn't sewing machines they made in that sinister place. It was something quite different.

It was a liquid—as Dr. Fetlock now explained—that you could spray onto ghosts so as to destroy them completely and forever.

"We have to keep our work secret," he told Fulton Snodde-Brittle. "That story in the paper did us a lot of harm. You see there are feeble and soppy people about who might make a fuss. They might think that ghosts have a right to be around and then there would be questions asked and laws passed. So I have to tell you that everything you see and hear in this building is top secret. Will you promise me that?"

"Oh yes, yes indeed," said Fulton. He had wasted no time in coming to see the doctor. "I'd rather not have my part in this talked about either. In fact, I'd like it if your men could come and spray Helton under cover of darkness."

"There shouldn't be any problem about that. Now, you will want to know what you are getting for your money, so let me show you round." Dr. Fetlock leaned forward and stared hard at Fulton with his black pop-eyes. His long hair straggled down his back, he wore thick glasses and looked as though he hadn't been in the open air for years. "But first of all, I have to ask you something: can you personally see ghosts? Are you a spook seer?"

Fulton stroked his mustache. A piece of kipper had caught in it from his breakfast, but he didn't know this and thought he looked good. "Well, actually, no. I can't."

Dr. Fetlock nodded. "Perhaps it's as well. But it means I'll have to explain the experiments to you. I will have to describe what we have done to the ghost animals we keep here so that you will see how amazing our product is. Now, if you will just put on this white coat, we will go into the laboratory."

He opened the door for Fulton and led him down a long dark corridor. "You will find that everyone here is really keen on their work. All the staff of EEB Incorporated—that's what we call ourselves—have suffered from disgusting spooks. The lab boy who is looking after the animals has a gash down the side of his cheek, as you will see. He got it when à head on a plat-

ter came out of the larder of his mother's house in Peckham. Just a severed head and nothing else—well, you know how these creepy-crawlies carry on. He fell over backward and gashed his cheek on the fire screen, and he's got the scar to this day."

"I'm sorry to hear it," said Fulton.

Dr. Fetlock opened the door of the animal house. What Fulton saw were rows and rows of cages with straw on the bottom and numbers nailed to the top. Beside the numbers were charts showing how much liquid the animals had been given and at what dose. A strange smell of decay hung about the room, and a murky fog clouded the windows.

"That's the dissolving ectoplasm," said Dr. Fetlock. "We'll get the fan going on it in a minute. Now, this top row is the rabbits. Of course we had to drill a small hole in their brains and squirt it with EEB—that's the name of our product—so as to destroy their willpower. Otherwise they'd just have glided through the bars—keeping ghosts caged up is the devil, as you know. The first three cages are the ones where we've destroyed the rabbits' left ears, and in the next row they've lost their right ears—it's a pity you can't see because it's a very neat experiment. Then below them we've got the mice. We've got rid of all the tails in the first batch and the second batch have got neither tails nor forepaws." He turned round and shouted: "Charlie!" and a youth in a spattered overall with a scar down the side of his face came out with a clipboard. "Show Mr. Snodde-Brittle the figures, Charlie."

Fulton took them and ran his eyes down the pages. They seemed to be graphs of different strengths of the EEB mixture set against the loss of limbs and ears and eyes.

"Very interesting," he said.

Dr. Fetlock had moved to another group of cages. "Now, these are the hamsters," he said. "You see we've managed to destroy their pouches completely. That's only the beginning of course . . . we're going to make the spray stronger and liquidate their front ends altogether so—"

"Yes, yes." Fulton was feeling a little queasy. "But how do I know it's going to work on humans? The ghosts I want to exterminate are people—well, they were."

Dr. Fetlock seemed to be thinking. "I think we'd best take Mr. Snodde-Brittle to the resting rooms, Charlie."

The resting rooms were just cubicles, rather like police cells, each with a camp bed, a gray blanket, and a water jug.

"Perhaps you'd like to look in here?" said Dr. Fetlock. "If you're sure it won't upset you."

"Nothing upsets me," blustered Fulton. He stared at the empty bed and the folded blanket—and saw nothing else.

"He was only a tramp," said Dr. Fetlock. "We thought it was quite right to use him for science. He was sleeping rough under Waterloo Bridge when he became a ghost. So we lured him in here—we said he could rest in peace and he *is* resting in peace!" He began to titter. "What's left of him!"

"Er . . . what is left?"

"A shoe with a broken sole . . . half a sock . . . look there, hanging over the bed. We came at him while he was asleep—three squirts from one of the big aerosols, and well, you'll see. We've got two more in the next rooms. The old bag lady is completely gone, but there's a drunk we found on the Embankment—his arms and legs have disappeared, but his torso's left, if you'd like to have a look."

"No, that's all right, thank you. I think I've seen enough," said Fulton. "But are you absolutely sure there's no effect on living people? I mean, I shall want to move back into the house when it's cleared."

Dr. Fetlock turned to Charlie. "Go and get Number Five. It's just been filled."

Charlie went away and returned with a large metal canister, rather like a fire extinguisher, with a hose and nozzle. The letters EEB were written on it in red paint. Dr. Felton put out his arm. "Right. You can give me a full dose."

Charlie pressed the nozzle. There was a hiss, and an

evil-smelling liquid shot onto the doctor's sleeve. Apart from the smell and a damp stain, nothing happened at all.

"Satisfied?" asked Dr. Fetlock.

Fulton nodded. "Yes, indeed. It's all exactly as I hoped. But . . . could one ask . . . what *is* EEB? What do the letters stand for?"

Charlie and Dr. Fetlock looked at each other. "Well, Mr. Snodde-Brittle, we don't trust everyone with this, but . . . all right . . . we'll take you along to the preparation room. It isn't I who discovered the EEB, you see—it's Professor Mankovitch. But I warn you, the Professor is completely mute. She's probably the most brilliant scientist in the world—a Hungarian; they're very clever in Eastern Europe—even the little children play chess—but she can't say a word. She lost her voice as the result of a frightful shock."

"What was that?"

"She was picnicking with her boyfriend in a forest. They have a lot of forests over there. And suddenly a whole lot of white, shimmering creepies came out of the trees—wibbly, wobbly, slithering ghoulies. They call them villis or tree spirits or some such thing. And they stretched out their awful arms and grasped her boyfriend and went off with him into the woods and he never came back. So she swore she would spend the rest of her life finding out how to destroy *things* that shouldn't be there. Come along, I'll show you."

Fulton followed him. As they came closer to the lab, he could hear a kind of bumping and gurgling, and the temperature rose. Then the door was thrown open and he saw an enormous vat that reached from the floor to the ceiling. A great piston went *thump, thump, thump,* stirring whatever was inside; tubes came from the vat and curled round the walls. Beside the vat, a woman with a blank face and white hair was twiddling a dial.

"This is it, Mr. Snodde-Brittle. This is the fruit of twenty years' work on the part of Professor Mankovitch. She has scarcely stopped to eat or sleep in all that time, but the result is success. Complete and total success. This vat is full to the brim of the most amazing discovery of the century. It is full, Mr. Snodde-Brittle, of EEB."

"Yes, but what *is* EEB? What's inside it?"

"You have heard of ectoplasm, surely?"

"Yes, of course."

"And you have heard of bacteria? Of germs? The things that cause measles and chicken pox and everything that's vile?"

"Yes."

"Well, we have found out how to grow a bacterium that eats ectoplasm. The Ectoplasm Eating Bacterium or EEB. We are manufacturing it as Rid-a-Spook and soon every hall, house, and mansion in the land will be free of ghosts!"

Fulton was convinced. He had come to the right

place. But when they were back in the office, he had a shock.

"How much would it cost to rid Helton Hall of ghosts? Completely?"

"Well, the charge is a thousand pounds a room. Which I'm sure you'll see is reasonable—"

"A thousand pounds a room! But Helton has got thirty rooms."

"Then it will cost you thirty thousand pounds. Which does not seem a lot to make sure that Helton is free of nasties forever. And I'm afraid I have to ask you to let me have the money in cash. You won't believe it, but we completely cleared a castle for a well-known British lord, and when we came to cash the check, it bounced."

Fulton was thinking, chewing on his mustache. How on earth was he going to get thirty thousand pounds? But once people knew that he was going to be the master of Helton, they'd lend it to him. After all, Helton wasn't worth thousands of pounds—it was worth millions.

"Very well, Dr. Fetlock," he said. "You shall have it in banknotes, I promise you."

. Chapter 21 .

ADDIE PERCHED ON the arm of the sofa and
glared at her long-lost parents. A night and a day
had passed since the Shriekers had seen the birthmark on Addie's arm and realized that she was their daughter, and the change in the evil pair was staggering. They
crawled about on the floor, they tried to touch the hem of
Addie's nightdress, they wept. And all the time they begged
and implored and beseeched their daughter to forgive
them.

"We shouldn't have done it," wailed Sabrina.

"We only meant to punish you a little. We didn't
think you would jump into the lake."

"We haven't had a moment's peace since that dreadful day we found that you were gone."

"That's why we tried to strangle other children. We
couldn't bear to see them well and happy while our
Little One was lost to us."

Addie took not the slightest notice. She had hung the

python, with his sad bulge in the middle, on the towel rail in the bathroom, and now all she cared about was helping Oliver. He *said* he was all right; he'd wanted to go out and fetch the clothes he'd left strewn by the lake the day before when he was helping Mr. Jenkins, but he still looked very pale, and the Wilkinsons insisted that he stay indoors and rest.

Aunt Maud would have been ashamed to moan and grovel like the de Bones, but she had never felt more wretched in her life. She felt sure that she was going to lose Adopta. Addie might say now that she was a Wilkinson, but how could she stand out against two such grand specters—specters with titles, who were from the upper classes? Sooner or later Addie would want to become Honoria de Bone, Aunt Maud was sure of that, and she felt as if her heart was breaking.

Uncle Henry and Grandma were almost as upset. They had known that they were only foster parents, but somehow they had not really thought that things would ever change.

All the same, Uncle Henry was a fair man, and now he said: "I think the de Bones must be allowed to tell their story. What was it that made Adopta jump into the lake and drown?"

So the Shriekers began.

• • •

"It happened on the night that Queen Victoria came to supper with us in our house near the Scottish border. You must remember our house, Honoria?" said Sabrina.

"I'm not called Honoria," said Addie, scowling, "and I don't remember a thing."

Sabrina sighed and went on with her story. "You have to understand how important it was to us to have the great Queen in our house. She was the Empress of India, remember, and the Mother of the Country, and it was her husband who first brought Christmas trees to England.

"So we prepared a tremendous banquet. We slaughtered seven oxen and shot one hundred and twenty pheasants and killed five dozen salmon and—"

"Well, I think that's disgusting," said Addie. "All those animals killed just to stuff into the stomach of a fat little queen."

"Yes, that's what you said. You were very angry. You were always an angry child—though we love you, of course. We absolutely adore you—"

"Go on with the story," said Adopta.

"So de Bone Towers was decorated with flags, and the crimson bedroom was hung with fresh tapestries, and there were flowers everywhere. It meant a lot to us, this day. You see, your father was expecting to be made an earl—people often were when they had the Queen to stay. But you had been getting crosser and crosser because of the dead animals. Of course, we quite understood but—"

Pelham put up his hand. "I will go on with the story," he said. "Queen Victoria arrived and we put on our evening clothes and our medals and our knee breeches. The footmen were in livery. The great hall sparkled with candlelight, and the table was set with gold plates and crystal goblets and decanters of priceless wine. Queen Victoria sat at the head of the table and the ladies-in-waiting sat at the foot of the table, and the pheasants were just being brought in on great platters—all one hundred and twenty of them—when the long windows onto the terrace opened . . . and a cow entered the dining room."

Addie was wrinkling up her forehead. "Daisy?" she said dreamily. "A cow called Daisy?"

"Yes, yes, yes!" cried Sabrina. "Oh, my little darling!"

"Go on," said the child. "What happened next?"

"Daisy was a large cow, ready for milking. She came up to the Queen and mooed and pushed her head onto the table and the glass fell over and spilled wine onto the royal skirt. Then came Buttercup . . . and after Buttercup came Violet . . . and after Violet came Rose and Geranium and Marigold. All our cows were named for flowers. Twenty-three cows were herded into the dining hall, mooing and shoving their heads into the plates and . . . er . . . lifting their tails to spatter the ground with manure . . . And after them came the bull. The bull was called Hector—he weighed over a ton—and he began chasing

Daisy. Daisy was his favorite. You can imagine . . . chairs turned over, people on the table, tails swishing . . . And the Queen, the famous Queen whose throne was inlaid with ivory and tourmaline and gold, shrieking and stepping in cowpats and being butted in the behind by Daisy's horns."

"And then came the sheep," said Adopta suddenly. "The cows were easy—I just shooed them up the steps— but the stupid dog couldn't get the idea of herding sheep *into* the house."

Both the de Bones turned to her. "So you do remember! It's all coming back to you," they said excitedly. "You see now that you are truly our child!"

Addie shrugged. "I remember the cows and the sheep— and that silly Queen honking at the end of the table."

"Anyway, that was the end of all Pelham's hopes of becoming an earl. The Queen left that night and never came back, and we were very, very angry. So we locked you in the tower at the edge of the lake. We just wanted to keep you there for the night and make you realize what a terrible thing you had done. We never imagined you would jump into the water and try to escape. Oh, the misery and the guilt and the wretchedness . . . After that I'm afraid we let ourselves go."

"You certainly did that," said Grandma, looking at Lady de Bone's dress and the bare feet with her moldering toes.

"Even before we became ghosts, we had become hermits in the castle," Sabrina went on. "And we decided that if our little girl was lost to us forever, no other children should sleep unharmed in their beds. But now everything will be quite different if only you will come into my arms and call me 'Mother.'"

"And come into *my* arms and call me 'Father,'" Pelham put in.

Addie twitched her nightdress out of his hand. "You must be mad," she said. "Do you really think I want parents who tried to kill my best friend? Not to mention what your beastly snake did to the budgie."

The de Bones sidled up to Oliver. "We are really very sorry, dear boy. Very sorry indeed," said Lady de Bone.

"On the other hand," put in Pelham, "you must remember that we were particularly *asked* to come here and do our most sinister haunting. We were *told* to go to the tower room and pull out all the stops. Mrs. Mannering said that the gentleman who ordered us most particularly *wanted* evil ghosts."

Everyone now looked at everyone else. The de Bones might be loathsome, but they seemed to be telling the truth.

Somone—and it had to be Fulton—had wanted Oliver harmed or even dead.

"*Now* do you believe me?" asked Adopta, turning to her friend.

But Oliver still had trouble believing that anyone who had sent him the Wilkinsons could be totally evil. "You don't think he guessed that the Shriekers were your parents and wanted to give you a surprise?"

"Oh for goodness' *sake,*" began Addie.

But she caught Uncle Henry's glance and said no more. Clearly something would have to be done about Fulton Snodde-Brittle, but not till Oliver could be got away to safety.

"Mr. Tusker thinks Oliver's drowned," said Eric when Oliver had fallen asleep at last. "I heard him going round the lake with Miss Match before he left. He's going to tell Fulton."

"Good," said Uncle Henry. "In that case, it won't be long before Fulton's back."

"And we'll be ready for him," said Sir Pelham. And this time the Wilkinsons were glad to hear the crack of his whip and see the hatred in his hollow eyes.

. Chapter 22 .

T O DECIDE THAT Oliver should be got out of
the way was one thing; to get him to go was
another. He didn't want to leave Helton even
for a couple of days. He knew how worried Aunt Maud
was about losing Adopta, and how Addie fretted about
the budgie, and he wanted to be with them and help.

It was Grandma who persuaded him to go. "I'm worried sick about Mr. Hofmann," she said. "And if you
mean it, I'd like to ask him down to Helton—and
Pernilla, too. But I want you to come, too, so it'll seem
like a proper invitation."

What Grandma started, Oliver's old friend Trevor
finished by writing to ask Oliver if he'd come to the
Home for his birthday. So they took the housekeeping
money that Miss Match had left in the kitchen drawer
and set off for London, and everyone in the Home was
so pleased to see Oliver, and so excited to have a ghost
to stay, that the boy couldn't be sorry he had come.

Now they were on their way to Mr. Hofmann, but there was something Grandma wanted to show him first.

"Here we are," she said. "This is the place."

Oliver stared through the plate-glass windows at the knicker shop.

"Is this really where you lived?" he asked. "Honestly and truly?"

"Honestly and truly," said Grandma. "Eric slept up there above the bikinis and Henry was in with the Footsies and we put Adopta in the office—that's through that door there."

Oliver was amazed. "I didn't realize it was so small."

"Small and stuffy and daft," said Grandma, snorting at the Wonderbras. They crossed the arcade and made their way toward the bunion shop.

Mr. Hofmann sat in his wheelchair as he had done every day for years. His eyes watered, his chest wheezed, his head wobbled. Above him was a picture of a stomach with lumps on it. Bowls for spitting into and rubber tubes for pushing down people's throats and packets of bandages were piled round him. The leather bunion was still there, but dusty, and Mr. Hofmann was extremely sad.

Then the door opened and a boy came into the shop. He was a nice boy and he looked healthy and Mr. Hofmann was sure he had come to the wrong place. But the boy came forward and smiled and said: "I've got a surprise for you!"

And then there she was, slowly becoming visible, his dear friend, the only woman who understood him and his suffering! There were the cherries trembling on her hat, there were the kindly wrinkles, the umbrella . . .

"Is it you?" croaked the specter. Tears sprang to his eyes; he tried to get out of his chair. "Is it really you?"

"Now, Mr. Hofmann, you've let yourself get in a dreadful pother," said Grandma. "Just look at you, you're the color of cheese and you shouldn't be sitting under that stomach, I told you before."

"Ah yes . . . but I am so weak . . . I am so useless . . . what matters it if I sit under stomachs or no."

"It matters a great deal," said Grandma sternly. "And now listen, because I've come to take you away. This nice boy lives in a beautiful house in the country and he's invited you down to live with us. For good."

But Mr. Hofmann only shook his withered head. "No," he said. "Such things do not happen to old useless German professors who are dead. I shall stay here alone and suffer. It is my fate."

But Grandma wasn't having any of that. "That's quite enough, Mr. Hofmann. I'm coming back the day after tomorrow to take you down, so make sure you're ready. Pernilla's invited, too, so we'll make a party of it."

They found the Swedish ghost drooping over her harp in the music store. She was overjoyed at the thought of living where there were forests and fresh, clean air, but she was worried about the jogger. They had become friends and tried to Keep Fit together, and she felt bad about leaving him alone.

Of course Oliver soon settled that. "He can come, too, honestly," he said. "There's plenty of room." And the smile that came over her face was wonderful to see.

When they got back to the Home, Grandma thought she might have a little lie-down or perhaps have a go with the Space Invaders game she learned the day before, but it didn't turn out like that. The children clustered round her and pestered her for stories.

"Tell about the time you held down the Nazi parachutist with the tip of your umbrella," said Trevor.

"And the one about how you pushed Mrs. Ferryweather into a flower bed because she wouldn't draw her blackout curtains," begged Nonie.

"And the one where the bomb fell and you found you were a ghost," said Tabitha.

"Yes, tell about that," cried all the children. That was their favorite.

Oliver, meanwhile, had been called into the office, where Matron and the two agency ladies had been having a meeting.

Miss Pringle and Mrs. Mannering had been frantic when they heard that the Shriekers had gone to Helton. They thought that if anything had happened to Oliver they would have to shut the agency and go and save whales or start a cat shelter, so when Grandma called in and explained that Oliver was safe, they were overjoyed. But, like Matron, they did not feel that Oliver should be at Helton with only the ghosts to protect him from Fulton Snodde-Brittle.

"Of course we could get hold of the police," said Matron. "But it's a strange story, and suppose we hit on someone who doesn't believe in ghosts? There's no doubt in my mind that Fulton's a villain, but you can't really arrest someone for giving a home to spooks. I think we must somehow keep Oliver here till his guardian comes. That lawyer seems to be worse than useless. It's monstrous that the boy should have been alone there without an adult all this time."

"Is there no news of the Colonel yet?"

"Well, yes. I sent a fax to the British consul in Costa Rica and it seems he's on his way back to Britain. Till then, Oliver will be safe here, and the children will love having him."

But when she told Oliver what had been decided, he shook his head. "I can't stay away that long; I just can't. Helton's my home now and Addie needs me."

Matron looked at his troubled face. "Yes, I quite understand that, Oliver. Look, would you stay till Trevor's party? It's only a few more days and it would mean a lot to him."

Oliver nodded. It meant letting Grandma go ahead

with the ghosts, but Trevor had always been his special friend.

"Yes, I'll do that," he said, and Matron was relieved. If Colonel Mersham had not returned by then, she would try to find someone to go to Helton with Oliver.

When he went back into the garden, Oliver found the other children still sitting listening to Grandma, but Trevor had left the circle and was waiting by the climbing bars. Trevor was tough: he'd had to be, losing his parents, losing one hand, finding that his relatives in Jamaica didn't want him. He was a boy who hit out first and asked questions afterward. But when Grandma came to the bit of her story where they'd found out that Trixie wasn't with them, he always got a lump in his throat. That poor spook in her flag lost in space forever . . . It was more than anyone could stand.

"I'm staying for your party," said Oliver. "But after that I'll have to go even if Matron doesn't give me permission. I'll have to."

Trevor nodded. "Maybe I'll come with you," he said.

. Chapter 23 .

THINK OF ROAST KIDNEYS dipped in icing sugar," said Adopta. "Or marshmallows fried in chicken fat. Go on, think of them," she ordered the snake.

But the python didn't. He was still draped over the toweling rail, and he wouldn't be sick no matter what she said to him. She could see the bulge where the budgie was, and since the python had swallowed him whole, she was hopeful that he might be all right, like Jonah inside the whale, but whatever she said to the wretched snake, he just hung there with a blank look in his eye, refusing to throw up.

Addie had spent a lot of time in the bathroom since the Shriekers arrived, because her long-lost parents were driving her mad. They popped up behind bushes begging her to call them "Mother" and "Father," or crawled about in the flower beds asking her to forgive them. Sabrina called her "Little One," and Sir Pelham wanted her to sit on his knee. But what made Addie really angry was the way they kept on snubbing the Wilkinsons. They called Uncle Henry "that tooth puller" and sneered at Eric's Pathfinder badge, and they thought it terribly funny that Aunt Maud had been a Sugar Puff.

And she was missing Oliver badly. She knew it was right that he should be out of the way till they had dealt with Fulton, but life was not the same without her friend.

Uncle Henry now came in, as he had done each morning, to look at the snake.

"I could operate, I suppose," he said, "but there's always a risk."

"Let's wait a bit longer," said Addie. She was cross with the python, but it was hard to think of a hole being cut into his side. "I'll go and see if Mr. Jenkins wants any help."

It was the farmer who was in charge of making it look as though Oliver had drowned. He saw to it that Oliver's shoes bobbed up occasionally, and that there were footprints leading into the water such as might be made by a boy running in terror from something evil. Mr. Tusker had been quite certain that Oliver lay at the bottom of the lake, and the ghosts were sure that Fulton would think the same.

But when she reached the water, Addie found Lady de Bone dripping bloodstains onto Oliver's torn shirt, and at once the fuss began.

"Ah, there you are, darling Honoria," she cried, trying to rub her nose stump against Addie's cheek. "Have you come to tell your mother that you love her?"

"And tell your father that you love *him*?" said Pelham, rising from the bullrushes.

"No, I have *not*," said Addie. "Where's Aunt Maud?"

The de Bones looked at each other. "She's in the walled garden smelling the flowers." Lady de Bone sneered.

But Aunt Maud was only pretending to smell the flowers. What she was really doing was trying not to cry.

"Have they been beastly to you?" asked Addie. "Because if so—"

"No, no. Not really. It's just . . . I mean, it's very silly of me not to know what a lobster claw squeezer is, but you see we never had them at Resthaven. And I didn't realize it was common to say 'toilet.' One should say, 'loo,' but I never have, Adopta. And honestly, I think it might be better if I just gave up and let them have you. I'm not really grand enough to haunt a place like this."

"Now, Aunt Maud." Addie was very cross indeed. "That's enough. If I've told you once I've told you a thousand times that I'm a Wilkinson. You and Uncle Henry are the only parents I want, and if they go on sneering at you, I'll do them in."

But when they started to rehearse the attack on Fulton and Frieda, even Aunt Maud had to admit that the Shriekers were impressive. When they stopped groveling to Adopta and did their proper haunting, the de Bones were something to watch. It wasn't just the flickering tongues of light and the evil stench with which they kept tradesmen and passersby from coming to the Hall. Sabrina could raise her skinny arms and decayed owls came tumbling down the chimney in droves, and when Sir Pelham cracked his lethal whip, the hardiest ghost felt his ectoplasm crawl and shrivel on the bones.

And since they expected to ambush Fulton by the lake when he came to make sure that Oliver was dead, they had their special outdoor effects. They could make great branches crack and fall; they could bring up a swirling fog that would blind any man, and call up shapes that writhed and snatched and gibbered in the undergrowth. The Wilkinsons meant to help, of course, but when it came to punishing Fulton Snodde-Brittle once and for all, they couldn't do without the Shriekers.

But it wasn't Fulton who came next to Helton Hall.

The ghosts were all in the drawing room having a sing-along. Grandma had brought Mr. Hofmann to Helton the day before, with Pernilla and the jogger, and he'd been resting ever since, but Aunt Maud thought they should have a bit of a party to show him how welcome he was. He couldn't eat—his intestines had gone completely to pieces in the bunion shop—but he loved music. Pernilla knew some splendid songs about mad trolls and screaming banshees, and though she would rather have been outdoors roaming in the woods, she stayed and sang to them in her lovely mournful voice.

Of course the Shriekers thought that sing-alongs were vulgar—they didn't have them in de Bone Towers—but that didn't mean they stayed away and left the Wilkinsons in peace. Even the farmer had come up from the lake. Only the ghoul still slept on his tombstone in the church. Every other ghost at Helton was gathered in that room.

No one looked out the window. No one saw a red van with some dreadful words painted on the side draw up in front of the house. No one saw the people who got out: a woman with white hair, a youth with an ugly scar on his face, and a man with pop-eyes and long black hair.

No one saw what they took out of the van: hose pipes with nozzles, face masks, canisters of liquid gas . . . no one saw anything until the door opened—and then it was too late.

. Chapter 24 .

IS THIS ALL YOURS, honest?" asked Trevor as he
and Oliver made their way up the drive. The roof
and towers of Helton in the sunrise looked like an
ogre's castle in a book. "No wonder you didn't want it.
What a pile!"

Oliver didn't answer. Now that he was back, he was
wondering why he'd been in such a panic to come home.
It had come over him suddenly after Trevor's party, the
feeling that his ghosts needed him. That night in bed it got
so strong that he'd started to dress almost without thinking. He'd meant to creep out alone and take the night
train, but Trevor had ears like a lynx. It was horrid, deceiv-
ing Matron, but nothing could have stopped Oliver.

But why had he felt like that? Everything was peaceful and quiet.

"They're probably still asleep," he said, and pushed
open the big oak door.

It was *very* peaceful and *very* quiet. Addie would probably be in the bathroom, trying to make the python sick, and Uncle Henry would be doing his exercises. He liked to get through them before Aunt Maud got up and told him not to strain himself.

Was it *too* quiet?

"There's a funny smell," said Trevor.

Oliver had noticed it, too. A sweet, sickly smell, drifting down the shallow marble steps toward them.

"Best prop the door open," said Trevor, and tugged at the heavy bolts.

Oliver did not help him. He was walking like a zombie toward the drawing-room door. He had reached it and somehow . . . opened it.

The ghosts were inside, all of them. And they were asleep. Oliver said this aloud so as to make certain that it was true.

"They're sleeping," he said to Trevor.

He wouldn't ask himself why they were lying like that . . . like sacks waiting to be dumped . . . like those piled-up bodies he had seen in pictures of war.

Trevor put an arm round his friend's shoulders. He'd known at once what Oliver would not admit: that something was terribly wrong.

They began to move about among the ghosts, to call them.

Not one of them stirred. Not one of them opened their eyes.

Grandma lay under a carved wooden table. Mr. Hofmann's sad old head was in her arms; she must have tried to shelter with him under the table like people did in air raids. But what had happened here was nothing as simple as a bomb.

Eric had slithered to the ground beside his father, and both of them had brought their hands up to their foreheads in a salute, as if they wanted to meet what was coming like soldiers or like Scouts.

Only what *had* come? What had turned this room into a battlefield?

Aunt Maud lay close to her husband, her face turned toward him as it always was when she wanted comfort. Oliver picked up her hand and felt none of the lovely, slithery lightness he was used to. It felt heavy and curdled, and when he let it go, it dropped like a stone.

"I can't bear it," said Oliver, and gritted his teeth because he was feeling sorry for himself and there might be hope still, and something he could do.

He moved on to Sir Pelham. If anyone could survive an attack it would be him . . . but when he turned the hairy, pockmarked face toward him, the head lolled back and the sightless eyes were like black pits of nothingness.

"It's to do with that smell, I'm sure," said Trevor. "If we could get them outside into the air . . ."

But Oliver had found Adopta. She lay between Aunt Maud and Lady de Bone, and both specters had stretched out their twisted limbs toward her as though even in their final agony, they'd fought for her. No, he'd got that wrong. Their arms were sheltering her, not grasping. They had made an arch round Addie's head; they had had time to make their peace.

Oliver knelt down beside his friend. The sponge bag had dropped from her fingers; her tumbled hair was spread out in a halo behind her head. She was so frail that he could make out the pattern of the carpet beneath her shoulders.

"Addie, you can't go away, you *can't*. I need you so much. Remember all the things we were going to do? Please, Addie, *please*."

As he tried to call her back, to prop her up, his tears fell on her upturned face. But nothing woke her, and to Oliver, suddenly, it was as though the end of the world had come. Everything bad that had happened to him: his parents dying, the year he had been shunted between people who didn't want him . . . everything got him by the throat.

"It's my fault," he sobbed. "It's because I went away and left them." And then: "I don't want to live."

Trevor had been trying to comfort him. Now he got up and tiptoed to the door. "Listen," he whispered. "Someone's just come in. Two people. I can hear them talking."

. . .

Fulton and Frieda stood in the hall at Helton and gloated.

"We've done it! We've got rid of the spooks and Oliver is dead! Helton is ours, Frieda! It's ours. It's ours!"

But Frieda had stopped at the bottom of the stairs.

"Are you sure it's safe? They're all done for, the creepy-crawlies?"

"Of course it's safe. You heard what Dr. Fetlock said when I handed over the money. 'Wait till morning to make sure their ectoplasm's properly eaten and then you'll be fine,' he said. And anyway the Ectoplasm Eating Bacterium doesn't hurt living people. I've told you."

"No. But I don't want to bump into half-chewed legs and fingers and things. Even if we can't see them, we might feel them. And there's a funny smell."

"Now, Frieda, you're always whining. The spooks are done for, and Oliver is dead! There's nothing to stop us now. Nothing."

"Yes, Oliver is dead—" began Frieda. Then she stopped and pointed with a trembling hand toward the top of the stairs. "It's his ghost," she said with chattering teeth. "It's Oliver's ghost!"

It was something anyone might have thought. Oliver was as white as a specter and he held something that real boys do not often hold: a great throwing spear with a black wooden handle and a point as sharp and lethal as only the warriors of southern Africa could make it; an assegai that he had plucked from the wall and carried as if it weighed no more than Grandma's umbrella.

And he had gone mad. Trevor saw that at once. This slight shy boy stared down at Fulton with such hatred that the Snodde-Brittles stood hypnotized like baboons in front of a leopard.

"I am not dead, as you see," said Oliver. "But you will be in a minute because of what you have done to my ghosts."

He lifted the spear and began to walk down the steps— and Fulton took a step backward and fell over Frieda, so that both of them rolled down onto the marble floor.

"I, too, am a Snodde-Brittle," said Oliver, still in that level voice. "And I Am Going to Set My Foot on *My* Enemies. *Now.*"

He took another step and lifted the spear, and as Fulton and Frieda tried to disentangle themselves, he brought the point down to touch Fulton's throat.

"No!" screamed Fulton. "Stop! I didn't mean it. I'm sorry! Don't kill me, don't!"

"But I'm going to," said Oliver. "I'm just looking for the best place."

Trevor had come round behind him. "Here, steady, Oliver. They'll put you away if you kill him, and you don't want that."

Oliver didn't even hear him. He brushed the tip of the

spear against Fulton's throat, and the scratch filled up with blood. No, not Fulton's Adam's apple—his heart . . .

Frieda was trying to scramble to her feet, but Trevor moved toward her and kicked her hard in the shins. If he couldn't stop Oliver, at least he could see that the woman didn't run away and squeal.

Fulton was grasping his throat, screaming with terror as his hand came away dipped in crimson.

Then from somewhere above them there came a . . . fluttering . . . the sound, faint as breath, of wing beats. And then a noise so unbelievable, so absolutely amazing, that Oliver couldn't believe his ears.

He turned his head only for a moment, but in that moment, Fulton and Frieda took to their heels and ran.

. Chapter 25 .

THE VAN WAS back in the garage. The letters RID-A-SPOOK had been painted out; it was just a plain red van now.

And the laboratories had been dismantled. The cages where the phantom mice had had their tails removed by the dreaded EEB had been sent back to the pet shop from which they had come; the resting rooms in which the tramp and the bag lady had been destroyed were once again ordinary cloakrooms.

"That should see it through," said Dr. Fetlock, who wasn't a doctor at all but plain Bob Fetlock, a man who'd failed every exam he'd ever taken but had a flair for tricking people.

"Six months in the sun!" said Professor Mankovitch, throwing her white wig onto the table and combing out her frizzy red hair. Her name was Maisie; she was Fetlock's girlfriend, and they were off to Spain.

"What a sucker that bloke was," said Charlie. His scar was real enough, but he certainly hadn't got it when a head on a platter came out of his mother's larder in Peckham. He'd got it by roller-skating into a milk truck when he should have been at school.

They'd worked on all sorts of scams, Fetlock and Maisie and Charlie, who was Maisie's nephew, but they'd enjoyed this one particularly.

"That was good, the bit about the villis luring my boyfriend away in the forest. I really went for that," said Maisie, lighting a cigarette. "Can you see me just sitting there while these white ghoulies knock off a bloke I fancied. I'd have kicked them in the teeth."

"It's a pleasure to deceive such a nasty piece of work," said Fetlock, who hadn't cared for Fulton Snodde-Brittle. "Swallowing all that stuff. Ectoplasm Eating Bacteria! What a twerp!"

Fetlock had got the idea out of a horror comic and set the whole thing up. There hadn't been any phantom mice or rabbits or ghostly tramps, of course. The labs that Fulton had been shown round were completely empty and the great thumping vat that "Professor Mankovitch" had been working on was left behind from a steam laundry. As for the stuff they'd squirted from their nozzles, it was a job lot of laughing gas they'd nicked from the back of the dental hospital. No one used it now for pulling teeth; it put people to sleep all right, but it made them so sick and silly and giggly afterward that dentists had stopped using it.

"Well, that's it, then," said Fetlock. "Thirty thousand in cash should keep us out there for a bit. Got the tickets, Maisie?"

Maisie nodded and shut her suitcase. "What'll happen to the spooks, do you reckon?" She was a person who could see ghosts, but she didn't care what became of them—she'd have done anything for money.

Fetlock shrugged. "Same as happens to people, I suppose. Only with them being sort of looser and woozier than us, the gas'll get further into their brains. All the same, we'd best be well clear of Fulton before they come round."

And ten minutes later, the premises of Rid-a-Spook were deserted . . . and as silent as the grave.

. Chapter 26 .

DO I LOOK all right?" asked Lady de Bone.

"Yes, Mother, you look fine," said Adopta. She rearranged a piece of liver in the specter's tangled hair and pulled her bloodstained skirt straight.

"What about me?" asked Sir Pelham. "Does my hoof-mark show up properly?"

Addie stood on tiptoe to examine the place where the horse had bashed in her father's head, and said they both looked fine and everyone would be terrified and now it was time to start.

The de Bones were always a little nervous before the doors of Helton opened to the public and the long lines shuffled in to see the Most Haunted House in Britain. The visitors liked seeing Mr. Hofmann's withered head coming out of the dining-room sideboard, and they enjoyed Grandma whooping up and down the window curtains, but it was the Shriekers who made them go

"Ooh" and "Ahh" and hold on to each other in terror and feel that they had got their money's worth.

It had been Oliver's idea to open Helton to the public so as to get money for the work he wanted to do, and it was a great success. Trevor was in charge of the car park, and Oliver showed people round, and Helton had already beaten all other stately homes for attracting visitors.

Three months had passed since Oliver had turned his head and seen the budgie giggling and laughing and falling about, and he and Addie were close now to fulfilling their dreams. Colonel Mersham had come to live at Helton and Matron had sent her sister down to keep house, and you couldn't have found two nicer people anywhere. As for Fulton and Frieda, no one had seen them since they scuttled away in terror from the Hall.

The awful moment when the ghosts saw the nozzle of the EEB people come round the door and believed they were finished had changed them all. In that ghastly moment, Lady de Bone and Aunt Maud had stopped fighting over Addie and sheltered her, and when they regained consciousness, the de Bones realized how wicked they had been and glided off to Larchfield Abbey to ask the nuns for forgiveness.

When they returned, a sensible arrangement was made about Addie. She spent the weekend with the de Bones, learning to say upper-class things and keeping her shoulders straight, and the week with the Wilkinsons, so that

she stopped being a tug-of-war ghost and became a ghost with two families, which is a very different thing. And if she was always glad when Monday morning came round and she could be a Wilkinson again, she kept these thoughts to herself.

With the money they got from visitors, Colonel Mersham and Oliver turned the stables into a Laboratory for the Study of Ghostliness. The Colonel was in charge of the work, with Uncle Henry to help him, and they made a splendid team. Already Helton was becoming the place to go if one wanted to know about ectoplasm and how it worked.

But the rest of the buildings and the gardens and the grounds filled up with Addie's pets. Every phantom animal who did not understand what had happened to it was welcome and not one was turned away: not the ghost of the meanest water flea or the skinniest tapeworm or the most beaten-up rabbit or the pigeon with gunshot wounds in its side. The duckbill in the zoo passed on at last, and Addie brought it down to live in the shrubbery, and though she never found a phantom sheep, she became quite fond of the python, who had been ill for a long time after the gas made him throw up the budgie and needed careful nursing. And there was one animal so special and so famous that scientists came from all over the world to see it sitting by the fountain: the shining, pop-eyed, and beautiful ghost of the golden toad that Colonel Mersham had brought back from the cloud forests of Costa Rica.

If Addie never turned away an animal in need, Oliver opened his home to every human spook without a place to lay his head. He had told the ladies of the adoption agency to send him any ghosts they couldn't place themselves, and soon the Hall was filled up with bloodstained widows and actresses who had fallen through trapdoors and foolish people who had thrown themselves under trains for love.

There was one ghost, though, who did not appear.

However much they called her, poor Trixie never came to them. But one night as they were gathered round the sundial for the Evening Calling, a specter did appear. A blowzy, raddled old spook with a puffy face and an out-of-date hairstyle who landed with a bump on the sundial.

"Coo-ee!" she called, waving a fat arm. "It's me. Don't you remember me, Eric? It's Cynthia Harbottle!"

It was the most incredible shock. Eric couldn't believe it. He'd remembered her the way she was, of course, a thin girl in a gym slip with marvelous teeth.

"I told you," said Aunt Maud under her breath. "I told you she'd be old."

Eric was speechless. He knew that if you love people you have to do it for always, and perhaps he would have tried, but then Cynthia did the most awful thing. She snatched Trixie's banana, peeled it—*and threw the skin onto the neatly swept gravel path.*

That finished it. No Boy Scout could ever bring himself to love a person who litters, and in that moment Eric's passion for Cynthia Harbottle shriveled and died.

Fortunately, she was only passing, and after she went Eric was a new man. He whistled as he worked, he went for long tramps in the woods, and when Oliver's friends came down from the Home for the holidays, he showed them all the clever things he had learned to do when he was a Scout: how to make a noise like a partridge, how to splice ropes, and which kinds of sticks are suitable for skewering sausages and which are not.

"I expect Frederica Snodde-Brittle would be just as awful if she turned up now," he said, trying to cheer up the farmer, and Mr. Jenkins had to agree.

• • •

It was just six months after the Rid-a-Spook people had been to Helton that Miss Pringle and Mrs. Mannering had a visitor who absolutely amazed them.

"You cannot be serious," said Mrs. Mannering when the ghost who stood before them told them what he wanted. "You want *us* to find you a home?"

The spook nodded. He had been an ugly man and he

was a hideous ghost, with his long, gloomy face and messy mustache and tombstone teeth. Not only that, but his forehead was peppered with gunshot wounds.

"I'm a ghost, aren't I?" said Fulton Snodde-Brittle. "I've got my rights, same as everyone else."

"No, Mr. Snodde-Brittle, you have *not,*" said Miss Pringle. She was a gentle woman, but she was absolutely outraged. "You have lied and cheated and been a criminal spook-destroyer and you are not a person we would ever have on our books."

"Well, I don't think that's fair. My sister ratted on me—she's gone all soft, and I can't go on living rough on my own."

The ladies knew what had happened to Frieda Snodde-Brittle. She had been so terrified when she saw Oliver's ghost that she had decided to stop being wicked and become a nun, and now she was living at Larchford with her head shaved, doing humble things like mucking out the stables and scrubbing floors.

As for Fulton, when he found out that the EEB people had cheated him and that Oliver's spooks were not only well and happy but making him rich, he went quite mad. He found an old gun that his father had used for shooting rabbits, and took off for Spain to find Fetlock and force him to give back the thirty thousand pounds.

Fetlock and Maisie were in a disco when Fulton stormed in and started shooting off his gun. When he had shot three strobe lights and a potted palm tree, he tripped over a bongo drum, and the gun went off and shot him through the head.

"I didn't ask to be a ghost," said Fulton, who had been sent back from Spain in a body bag. "I hate the things. But here I am and I want somewhere to live."

Miss Pringle and Mrs. Mannering turned to each other. Their eyes met. They smiled.

"Well, Mr. Snodde-Brittle," they said, "there is one place that might just suit you."

So that's where Fulton landed up . . . among the bikinis and the see-through nighties and the Footsies in the knicker shop.

Oliver goes to visit him sometimes when he and Matron's sister go to London, but it's a waste of time. Fulton just rants and raves among the underwear and tries to tear the Wonderbras to pieces with his teeth.

• • •

But for the Wilkinsons, the people who had made him so happy and become his family, Oliver had a most wonderful surprise in honor of their first year at Helton.

Aunt Maud had tried to share the Hall with the Shriekers, and not to worry when it was Addie's turn to be with them. But though they behaved so much better, they were still very snooty, and she never felt really at home among the huge knobbly furniture and the brown pictures of things being shot and the heavy fire irons. Oliver had seen this, but it wasn't till the farm turned a profit and he'd done some accounts with his guardian that he saw what to do, and it was really very simple.

He rebuilt Resthaven in the gardens of Helton Hall. He built it exactly as it had been, with the bow windows and the stained glass in the bathroom and the pretty porch. He had the door painted blue and the bird table with the rustic roof put up beside it, and he found a mat with WELCOME on it just like the one that had been there before.

So just fifty years after they lost their beloved home, the Wilkinsons moved into it again. And this time no bombs fell from the sky, and the country was at peace.